Harry Moon

The Blue **Eyed** Wolf

Elizabeth Johnson

ISBN: 9780995471184

London

I dedicate this book to God Almighty for the inspiration, love, and the confidence He gave me to pursue my heart's desires. Thank you, my Father, for your unfailing love.

To my family, especially three wonderful boys, Josiah, Jesse, and Jaden who encourage me every day to follow my passion.

And to all those that read my previous works and nudged me forward with their amazing reviews I thank you all for your endless support.

# Chapter 1

## Harry Moon

"Ahhhhh!!!" I heard my mum screaming out for help as I was being pushed down in her belly. Then another groan, and another agonizing scream; I thought my ears will damage as she yelled. I felt very uncomfortable, I had no control over what was happening, a force was pushing me downwards with every scream mum made. Then I felt a touch, it felt strange, a hand was pulling me out into the world and mum gave a final shout. Something was different; air rushed to my nostrils, and I felt cold as the air wrapped itself around my naked body. I tried to open my eyes, so I could see what was happening around me and a light like no other consumed my eyes, it felt like I had lived in darkness all my life. I started to hear a lot of talking, my mum was no longer screaming and I was no longer in that discomfort that consumed me earlier, just another type that made me feel weird. It felt odd, I didn't understand what just happened, why I was forced out of my home. I tried opening my eyes again. My mother cried softly. I could hear her relief as she said.

"Give him to me, let me see him, my little joy." I knew it was her; I could not mistake her voice for another, she sang and spoke to me in a whisper, as though she didn't want anyone else to hear what she had to say. I let out a soft cry, I wanted to speak but instead a strange sound came out of my mouth that didn't make sense to anyone. Mum laughed softly, and planted kisses on my face.

"Welcome, my little joy," she said. She looked at me, as I squinted my eyes, still trying to get used to the flood of light hammering my face, and my whole body in fact. Mum made a funny expression, I didn't know what it meant, she pouted her lips and made kissing sounds just like the ones she did when she kissed my face earlier. I tried to copy what she was doing; I saw her smile. I liked that; I made her smile.

"My baby, my Harry Moon," she said. I didn't understand what it meant then.

"Harry Moon?" A woman came close to us. "Is that baby's name mum?" she asked as she beamed down at me.

"Yes, his name is Harry Moon," Mum confirmed.

"Oh, what a lovely name, for such a beautiful baby," She remarked. "Is it okay if I take him for a little while?" she asked mum and I saw mum nod her head. I wanted to protest, I didn't want her to take me from my mother, we only just met really, I thought. "You're coming with me Harry Moon," the woman said with a funny expression planted on her face. I wondered if she knew how foolish she looked making faces at me. She took me from my mother's grasps.

"I'll see you soon darling, sooner than you think," Mum promised, she sounded weak.

"Yes, that's right. We just need to take a look at him, see that he is all okay. And you need to rest mum, you will need your strength for when we bring him back," she said. Her voice was different, it wasn't as consoling as my mothers.

"Where is she taking me?" I wanted to ask. "Don't let her take me away from you," I voiced, as my vocals opened into a cry. I didn't like being away from my mother. While I was in that dark space, I had gotten used to her voice; when she wasn't singing or speaking, I'd give her a little push to remind her I was still there, it made me safe and I didn't feel alone.

Soon, I was back in mum's arms. A few people came to visit, not many, they all made funny faces at me as their voices changed when they spoke to me, I wondered why they did that. Their voices were normal when they conversed with mum, why were they making annoying faces making their voices go high when they looked at me or spoke to me?

Soon mum and I were allowed to go home, and it was just us. We didn't have many visitors, mum was always around when I needed anything, all I had to do was cry and she would come running. Even when there was nothing wrong with me, Mum dropped everything to see I was okay once she heard me cry. I tried to be good for her, not to worry her so much.

As I grew, mum taught me everything she could, how to ride a bike, how to swim, she helped me with my homework and gave me a sticker each day I did something good. This was almost every day as I wanted more than anything to please her. I did my chores, tidied up my room, folded my clothes and studied hard to be the best in my class. I wanted my mother to be proud of me, because she gave me her best each day.

Everything was as it should be, except for the part where I have no dad and mum refused to talk about him to me. Still, life was good, until one day when I was thirteen. A new boy joined my class. I was the class ambassador so I went to him to introduce myself and make him feel welcome:

"Hello, I am Harry Moon, welcome to 8A, would you like to tell me your name?" I asked.

"My name's James Stein" he replied. I introduced him to all of my friends and from then on, James and I became good friends.

One day, we were on the playground, about three months after James joined my class. We just finished a quick football match with some of our other school friends. I was tired, and didn't want to play anymore. The rest of the boys ran rings around each other, they were being silly, around the playground. James came to me, to see if I was okay. I shrugged and told him; I was just not in the mood for rough play. He sat next to me, and we watched our friends tackle each other for a while and then out of nowhere he turned to me and said.

"Can I tell you something?"

I looked at him, "Yeah course, what is it?" I said returning my eyes to our friends.

"I am half human, half wolf," he blurted out. I didn't know if I should laugh or if I should take it seriously. "Yeah? Me too," I joked. I made to get up, the break was almost over and it was time to return to our class.

James held me back, I turned to face him. "Harry, Harry, I'm serious," he said, the look on his face told me he wasn't lying. If anything, I could always tell when my friends were not being truthful. I squinted, and shook my head in confusion. In my head, I thought if that was true, why was he telling me of all people. I wanted to ask him why he felt the need to tell me, but there was no time for that not now that the bell that signifies the end of break had rang. So, instead I said, "Okay James, I always knew you were special like that." I meant it when I said he was special. My mother always said we were all created specially by God, but that didn't mean I wanted to be involved in whatever secret he had going on in his life.

James smiled, "I always knew I could tell you anything. I have wanted to say that loud to someone for so long," he said in relief.

I faked a smile, as much as I was happy, he could unburden himself, I didn't think I was the right person to unload to. What was I meant to do with his secret now, I thought? I got up and began walking briskly towards the classrooms. James, walked along side me, keeping pace. I didn't want to look at him, but I didn't want him to think I was being weird I just needed a little time to process what he just said, that is if there was any truth to it. As I sat in my seat, James walked up to me, leaned into my ears and said.

"Thank you for understanding."

I smiled and nodded to acknowledge him. Focusing on the remaining lessons for the rest of the day proved difficult, I kept imaging him, turning into a wolf and killing my friends and my teachers.

Someone said something, and all heads turned towards me. By the time I realised, that the teacher was talking to me, someone had thrown a scrunched-up paper at the back of my head from the back of the class.

"Earth to Harry Moon," Mr Wyle said.

"I'm sorry sir, what was the question again?" I asked, and the whole class roared into laughter.

"You need to focus in my class and stop daydreaming if you don't want to get yourself into detention," he warned, and then moved on to someone else. I looked through the sea of faces still laughing at me, and saw James as his eyes penetrate mine. He must have known that his earlier revelation had done a number on me. That is if it was true. This could have been a prank he and the rest of my friends were playing on me.

"Are you all in all the joke too?" I voiced.

I saw James, shake his head in disagreement and disappointment. If eyes could kill, I thought, in his eyes was a glimmer of anger, as he thought I was about to reveal what he had shared with me with the rest of the class. In that moment, I believed he is truly half human half wolf

"Do you have anything to share with the class?" Mr Wyle asked.

My eyes moved from James to Mr Wyle, I shook my head, before attempting to speak. "No sir."

"Then shut your mouth and don't disrupt my class."

I nodded and tried to focus on the rest of the lessons.

When the bell rang to signify the end of the school day, I quickly grabbed my bag and ran home. I didn't want to talk to anyone let alone James. Mum would know what to do I thought, she will advise me, and tell me what to do about James' secret.

# Chapter 2

## Obsession

Since James' revelation about what or who he really is, I have been wondering what it must be like to be a wolf. I have wondered if all his family were wolves and if that were true, if they all can turn into full wolves at will. I wondered what he meant by half human half wolf.

When I got home from school on the day he told me his secret, I was set on telling mum, but just as I was about to tell, I saw an image of a wolf tearing my mum to pieces in my mind. The fear that by telling her, I could be jeopardizing her life, kept my mouth shut. Mum knew something was wrong with me, she could always tell. So, when she asked why my mood was not its usual jovial self, I kept the real truth of what troubled me to myself but instead, told her that Mr Wyle had humiliated me in school. She bought it, and I was relieved. After dinner, I quickly excused myself and headed for my room. If I stayed with her any longer, she would suss me out for sure and I would be forced to tell a secret that was not mine to share. However, the image of James hurting my friends or other people in the neighbourhood where he lives bothered me. I was working myself up, and it affected my sleep. I dreamt a wolf was stalking me, chasing me. It was really a horrid affair. For the next week, after James' revelation, he didn't show up to school. The official report was that he was ill, but all sorts ran through my mind.

Like, "Was he really ill, or had he just killed someone and needed time to dispose of the body." I had to see him and find out the real reason he was absent from school. If he admitted that he had killed someone, what then? It's not like he will allow me to go report him to the authorities. I thought about going to my class teacher and telling him what James had said, but then, I wondered about his family, what if they go after my mum and I. I couldn't risk her life that way, not in anyway.

My obsession for the truth consumed me. I started reading books on wolves, watching movies about them and searched the internet for information too.

Even at school, when James finally returned to class, I watched him, especially when someone angered him. I wondered how he was keeping it all under control. James could tell I was different with him now, I avoided being alone with him and I hated it. I hated that he told me his secret and I went all weird on him, but it's not every day one of your best friends tell you that he is half human half wolf; whatever that meant. If he could change at will if angered by some of our friends, then no one was safe. I was panicking inside. These thoughts disturbed me so much and I couldn't share them with anyone. Then I came to the conclusion that I couldn't avoid James forever, if there was any truth to what he said, only he could put my mind at rest and tell me that he wasn't a danger to anyone.

So, I summoned the courage to ask him at lunch that afternoon. I knew he wanted to speak with me too. I had felt his eyes on me all through the week. When I sat at the table, before our other friends came over, James came over with his tray. I looked from my food to his face. I could tell he was upset with me. Before I could speak, he said.

"You've been avoiding me."

I nodded, "Yes, I have, I just needed time to process everything…" I said in a low voice.

"And now, have you finished your processing?"

"No not really, I have questions."

"Okay, what do you want to know?"

"Why me? Of all our friends why tell me and burden me with your secret. I get that you needed to get it of your chest, but why tell me?"

He shrugged, "I don't know, I just felt in that moment that I could trust you." James responded.

"Okay, another question. Can you change into a wolf at will?"

He looked at me as though he was deciding if he had told me enough. Then he said, "Not here, I will find you later on the playground. We will talk more then."

I nodded as others joined our table. I pretended that everything was okay with us. I knew what he had to tell me later would help me decide what action to take next. I wanted to know what it was like to live life as half human, half wolf and how he managed to keep his real identity a secret. When playtime came, we had a game of it, and played a short football game with friends. Then I excused myself, I went to the toilet to pee, as I came out of the toilet, James was waiting for me. I was startled as first, then I remembered we had to talk.

"Let's talk," he said,

"Yeah! Let's talk." I repeated. We walked in silence to a bench at the end of the playground where we knew no one will disturb us. James sat next to me like he had done the day he revealed *who he was* to me.

"Harry, since I told you what I am, you've not been the same with me. I can see it has bothered you and I am sorry I did that to you," James apologised.

"Oh no! um, don't say that, I am glad you trusted me with this, I mean... I just want to ... you know... understand this whole wolf thing better." I gestured with my arms as I explained.

He looked at me, and then turned his attention on the rest of our friends that were running about. "You're worried, I will hurt someone or you?" James asked looking into my eyes for affirmation.

I tried to hide my concern but he could tell, I was really worried. "Can you blame me. I mean, wolves are dangerous, really, really dangerous. And you are one, I mean what is half human, half wolf anyway. Do you become some kind of werewolf or do you like turn into a real wolf?" I questioned. I felt my voice riding high.

"Hey! Keep your voice down. One thing you cannot do is tell anyone about this."

"Yeah, I know that, I will never tell anyone. I mean, I don't want to, not unless you are going about killing people for food." I said with panic in my eyes.

"Well, I don't do that," James responded, looking away from me. We were both silent for a while. I could feel he was remorseful that he told me. James turned to me. "Harry, I don't want you to worry; I will never do that, hurt our friends or anyone for that matter. I have learned to control my emotions so that when I am angry it does not bring out my other side. When I am human, I am just that, human and when I decide to become wolf, I can just be a wolf. Not the werewolf kind, a real wolf, but I still have my human emotions and understanding. I still know the people around me except if I decide to turn it off."

"Wow! That's pretty awesome. You mean you can decide to just live like an animal, how do you do that?" I asked in awe.

"That rarely happens, because, that will be dangerous for the people around me and I never want to do that. If ever, that happens, it will only be because I don't want to remember who I am anymore," James explained looking ahead at the other boys as they played. A ball was thrown in our direction and James got up to get the ball.

"James?" I called, he turned to face me. "I'm sorry I've been weird."

He smiled and went to join the others. I remained where I sat, thinking about what James had just said. I wondered what could happen that would make one not want to remember oneself.

The chat changed a lot for me. My perspective of James as a villain changed, and somehow, I began to want to be close to him. I had another level of respect for James now, living with such a secret and still keeping his head and not allowing his emotions to control him. I was no longer worried about

James losing his head when the boys poked
fun at themselves.

# Chapter 3

## The wish

Soon it was going to be my fourteenth birthday, and all I could wish for was becoming like James. I kept dreaming about how cool it would be to be able to just turn into a wolf and turn back into a human at will. Everything would still be normal; James lives with his father and it doesn't seem like having the wolf gene affected his family. I wondered what his mother would think of him becoming a wolf - as long as he still got to be in her life, it would be the greatest gift. Finally, my birthday arrived; I invited a few of my friends over to my house. Mum put up balloons, birthday banners, a lot of pizza boxes, burgers, sausages, donuts, crisps, sweets, popcorns, drinks and a big cake with a number 14 candle stuck in the middle. When it was time to blow out the candle and I was asked to make a wish, I shut my eyes and wished I could be like James but I knew it would never come true. None of my wishes had ever come true. In the past, my wish had always been wasted on my dad. Every birthday I wished that my father would come and visit, just for the day but for 13 years that wish was never fulfilled. Mum pretended, that my father had no significant contribution in my DNA. So, I thought, this time why waste my wish on someone that I never met, when I can wish to become someone that I now respect. But for once I hoped that the universe will give me what I want and make me a special boy like James.

All my friends had a parent with them at the party at Mum's insistence; James came along with his dad too. James' dad had a presence that was bigger than life. He helped Mum with anything she needed. And for a second, I wished that they would get together, so that James and I could become brothers. Suddenly a solemn feeling overcame me. Even though it was my birthday, and every one of my friends were here to celebrate with me, I felt like something was missing, like I wasn't complete. It couldn't be because I wanted what James had, it had to be more. I tried to look all excited for Mum and my friends but deep inside I felt empty. I wanted to be on my own so I went to my room and lay on my bed.

I began to play with the light switch beside my bed, switching it on and off, then I heard something. I got up from my bed and walked towards the door. I heard the sound again, like something was knocked off the table. The sound was coming from Mum's room; I walked slowly towards her room. Standing in front of her door, I heard something or someone tumble, or so I thought. I placed my hand on the doorknob to open it. As I was about to turn the doorknob, the door opened suddenly and James' dad stood in front of me. I was shocked. I didn't understand what James' dad was doing in Mum's room. For a second I had hoped that they will fancy each other but I wasn't expecting it to happen so quickly. Then, Mum appeared behind him and I became even more confused. I looked from James' dad to my mum and back to him before Mum finally spoke.

"Erm… Harry dear, erm… Mr erm…" she was struggling for words.

Without taking his eyes off Harry, James's dad said, "Mr Stein."

"Erm… Yes, Mr Stein was helping me change the light bulb. Anyway, what are you doing here lad, come on go play with your friends, it's your birthday," Mum bent down to kiss me, and I noticed a deep scratch on her arm. I looked at the scar and Mum pulled down the sleeves of her shirt to cover the scratch and looked at me and smiled awkwardly. It was obvious she didn't want me to talk about it. I knew what that look meant. I knew what all her looks meant. There was the one that says; "I am tired now Harry," the "don't you dare do that here Harry," the "what are you doing boy, you better stop it or there will be consequences" but this one was the "now is not the time" look. I understood it and I wasn't even in the mood to argue with her. I walked away and into a sitting room filled with screaming boys and girls. I stood by the door and just looked on. I didn't notice James until he was right next to me. "You don't look like you're enjoying your party," James commented.

"I know, I can't wait for the day to be over," I said, looking away from him.

"What did you wish for?" James asked and I turned to face him.

"What!" I voiced.

James continued, "You know when you blew your candle out, what did you wish for?"

I sighed, "Oh that." I paused for a moment, my gaze locked on James and then I finally said, "To be like you."

James' eyebrow lifted with surprise. "Really! that is what you wished for?" James asked confused.

"Yeah, but what are the odds right, it's never going to happen. I don't think that is how it happens right? One doesn't just wish for the impossible and it happens. Like with my dad, since I can remember I have wished that he would come looking for me one day. But I guess it's just a pipe dream. Just like me wishing to be like you."

****

(James's dilemma)

James looked away, he mused over what Harry had just said, he wanted to make Harry happy but he wasn't sure making Harry to be like him would make Harry happy. He debated with himself about what to do. He had already broken the first rule his dad gave him, not to tell anyone about their secrets and now here he was contemplating making Harry like himself. That is him breaking the ultimate rule.

But there was something about Harry that drew him to him, like they were already brothers, and if he did this, that will seal their brotherhood for life. But this could also kill Harry and he didn't want to risk that. The Wolf choses you, you don't just become it, if you don't already have the predisposition. But something about Harry felt right and James knew if he gave Harry the gift today, he would be giving him the ultimate gift and changing Harry's life dramatically.

James also knew how hard it was to adjust to the wolf's life, to control the emotion, the urge to kill, the urge to run free. This would be hard; it would be unfair to do that to Harry. James argued with himself but then again Harry was a good friend and James thought the least he could do was fulfil one of Harry's wishes. If he could make at least one of his wishes come true, then he had to try to make his friend happy he convinced himself.

****

We were both quiet just looking at the other kids partying, I was trying to get my head back together so I can enjoy the day when James spoke.

"I can make you like me, if that is what you want." James said his voice low, his eyes remained on the crowd.

I jerked my head towards him; I wanted to see his face, to see if he was serious, if he meant what he just said. I didn't want him toying with my emotions. "Can you really?" I asked in bewilderment.

James nodded; I could tell now that he meant what he just said but then I had to be sure.

"Really?" I asked and James nodded again. "How and when?" was what came out of my mouth next.

"Now if you like, but before I do it, you should know that this will change your life for good, and sometimes for bad. Do you still want it?" I nodded hastily. "Okay if I do it, we would be bonded for life, also there is the possibility that if the wolf doesn't choose you, it could kill you. This is very dangerous, are you sure you still want it?"

That took me a minute to process. "You mean, I could die in the process?"

James nodded, "Yes, but not exactly the minute I turn you. Perhaps when you first try to change, but if you survive, you will be stronger for it. If you are anything like I was, you won't suffer so much. It will be as easy as breathing when you change. Not the first time but every other time after."

I smiled, and thought about it for a minute. I had obsessed over this since the minute I knew of James' secret and now I had the opportunity to become one. I knew I had to take it. I may never get the chance again. I looked at Mum, she and James' dad were still flirting. I thought of all the possibilities of what would be once this was done. James and I will be bonded for life; we will become brothers. And if Mum and his dad hit it off, we could all become one big family and I will finally have a dad. I smiled at the thought of that future. I would love that very much. That didn't seem like a hefty price to pay, for some reason, I couldn't think of anything else or any other reason why I shouldn't become like James. I felt ecstatic that for the first time my wish would come true.

Finally, I looked at James, "Okay, you and I will be brothers for life," I pronounced. I smiled as I looked at the rest of the kids, no one seemed to mind that we were on our own, in our own world and for the first time that day, I felt happy. I felt like the missing pieces in my life was coming into place. Suddenly, while I was still distracted, James held my hands, one of his fingers turned into a claw, he dug it into my skin and scratched me deep. I winced in both surprise and pain. James looked at me and whispered, "Hold it together now, whatever pain you feel now, it will be worst through the night and then if you make it through, you will become like me."

I could feel the sweat gathering around my forehead as I tried to fight back the pain that shot through my hands. "I didn't think you meant right away," I grimaced.

"Why wait?" James added, "It's done, there's no going back now. I have to leave now. Get your mum to send everyone home, you need to be alone," he said, his tone was serious.

I knew I had to do what James said right away. I could already feel different inside, like something was beginning to grow inside me, and it needed every available space. I looked at the crowd of parents and children; I turned and saw James with his dad. James whispered something to his dad, his dad shot him a serious look, grabbed his coat and off they went. Before stepping out of the door, James shot me a look that said, get everyone out now. The pain became more intense. I turned towards Mum's room to ask her to send everyone away. The people in front of me were turning into doubles of themselves. I could barely hold it together, I staggered in pain as I walked towards Mum who met me in the hallway. "What's wrong Harry?" I heard Mum voice out.

"Is he alright?" I heard a woman say.

"I'm not sure," Mum replied. Mum held on to me. I looked in her eyes and saw she looked as bad as I felt or perhaps, I wasn't seeing anything clearly anymore.

"Harry Moon, look at me. I am sending everyone home now; I don't feel well my lad. Do you mind?" she asked. She didn't look good but she was doing her best to keep it together. She gave me a quick hug and walked me to my room, then as I got into bed, Mum pulled the cover over me. As she made to leave, I thought I heard her scream.

"Mum?" I called, my voice faint as the pain held on to me. Then she left for the living room, turned down the music.

"Alright everyone, thank you for coming. Harry needs to rest; he is a bit tired," she announced. I could barely hear what she was saying but people started to leave. A few friends poked their heads into my room to say goodbye before leaving. I managed a smile, pretending I was too tired but the pain was killing me inside, until finally everyone was gone and it was just me and Mum.

Mum came over to my room, I pretended as though I was sleeping. She ruffled my hair and staggered into her room. I didn't have the strength to ask her what was wrong with her, neither could I tell her what I had done to myself. Then I heard Mum yell in pain, it was pain I recognized very well, it sounded like when she was pushing me out of her belly. I didn't have the strength to sympathize with her as I was soon yelping out in terror myself. My bones felt like they were on fire, and breaking at the same time. For the first time, since James told me what he was, I wished that I had not wanted to be like James. I wanted to be my old self again.

Nothing was worth this much pain, I thought. Mum was going through her own terror, I didn't know why she was in pain, as I couldn't think past the pain consuming me. Then my body made another cracking sound and my eyes glazed over from the pain and I passed out. Only to wake to another agonizing pain and I felt like I was in hell for another hour with no one coming to my aid. Then, I heard Mum scream again, that was when I remembered the scratches on her arm, and James' dad standing next to her in her room. Could she be going through the same thing as I was? Could she have wanted this too? I couldn't dwell on it too much, as another dose of agony took all reasoning away.

# Chapter 4

## A reorganized life

Since my birthday, I have not gone back to school. I was happy to have made it to the next morning alive. My mother never asked me what happened to me since it meant she had to explain why she was screaming in pain all night.

My moods changed easily, I would get mad at her for keeping her distance from me and storm into my room and before I knew it, I would change from human into wolf. It scared me so much, so I remained in my room ashamed to come out until I calmed down and then my body like magic turns back into its human form again.

My mum was also getting very snappy with me, when I questioned her about things, she would snap and walk away from me. I knew we both had to address what was going on, we couldn't continue like this but Mum was never going to say anything.

I had not seen James or his dad since my birthday, it worried me. I wondered why he hadn't come to find me and check how I was doing. I know now that the scratch on my mother's arms came from his dad. My mum's erratic behaviours were like mine but I just didn't understand why she wanted to become a wolf.

A week passed since I was last at school; my mother called and told the school I was down with fever. Which wasn't a lie, my body's temperature was through the roof but I was getting used to it. The first three days were very bad; I was always pouring cool ice water over my body to cool the heat burning through me, Mum was apparently doing the same as we ran out of ice.

Mum finally came to find me in my room, I was pouring cold water down my head. I turned and looked at her.

"We need to talk Mum," I said.

"I know Harry Moon, it's time we both talked." "Something happened to us, I can tell that what happened to me happened to you," I said, she looked at me and tears formed in her eyes.

"I am sorry, I don't know what happened, I was just... I made a mistake. I just didn't like being alone all the time. I know I have you and you mean the world to me but I get lonely sometimes you know."

"What are you talking about? What happened to you, mum?" I asked, I wanted her to get to the point.

She paused and looked at me, "I was, I um… invited erm… you know the man erm… James' dad to help me fix the bulb and erm… we got carried away, I was leaning to get something and our eyes met, and I kissed him and he kissed me back and then I lost my footing and stumbled backwards and he tried to save me and as he made to grab me, his fingers dug into my arms and scratched me."

"James' dad scratched you accidentally!" I yelled out and she nodded.

"Then, he panicked when he saw the scratch, I didn't understand but he said, he was sorry that he should have been more careful and he said he had done something terrible to me and now I understand what he meant by that. Harry Moon, he turned me into a wolf," she said, tears clouded her eyes. "I don't feel the same again, my senses are heightened. I'm hungry all the time, snappy; I can't control my emotions. I'm scared I will hurt someone.

I can't go to work like this, the life I knew is over," Mum lamented.

I looked at her and wondered why this happened to the two of us on the same day even though I had wanted it, a decision I regret more than anything now but she didn't ask for this and here we are now. Now it was my turn to confess my sins.

"I am sorry Mum. I didn't know what being a wolf would cost. James told me months ago that he was half wolf, half human and since he revealed himself to me, becoming a wolf was all I could think about. And when you asked me to blow out my candle and make a wish, that was all I wished for. James asked me about my wish and I told him that I wanted to be like him. And now I regret ever asking him to make me a wolf because now I am one. I am a wolf just like you Mum and everything that is happening to you is happening to me," I confessed; Mum looked at me in shock.

"Oh! Harry Moon, why? Why would you want this? I can't even get angry because we are both the same thing now. Oh Harry, come here lad." I went over to my mum and buried myself in her embrace. "We will get through this I promise; we will learn to control it and live just like James and his father."

"What if we start to kill people? What if I get angry and turn outside? What if people find out and say we are monsters because we have become monsters, they will kill us." I asked my mum in hysterics.

"No Harry Moon, no one would dare, I will never allow anyone to hurt you. We will learn to control our feelings. We will learn not to get angry. We will continue to live our normal lives; no one will suspect anything but we have to start now, okay? My darling you have to return to school soon, but first I will take you to see a doctor. He will give us a note to cover all your absent days and I have to get back to work before people start asking us difficult questions."

I looked at her, and nodded, she believed what she was saying so I believed it too.

My mum took me to the doctors as promised. My body was boiling hot the doctor prescribed painkillers. On our way home, she dropped the doctor's note at my school to inform the school that I was still poorly so I am not expected at school yet until I was able to control my situation better. When we got home, she started to train me to control my emotions. She would say nasty things that would get me annoyed. At first nothing she said annoyed me because I knew it was my mother and she didn't mean any of it. Then she started to say things about my father; how he never loved me, how he never wanted me, how I don't mean anything to him, and that angered me. I felt a pain shoot through me and I changed my form. Then she walked towards me, I growled at her the closer she got. I towered above her, either that or she shrunk in size. Mum reached out her hand carefully and she sang me a song, her voice soothed me, and I felt my emotion begin to calm until the anger that anchored me disappeared.

A week passed, and we experimented with various things until I learned not to change my form when angered. We both didn't know what we were doing but we were doing the best we can with what we knew. We only had each other. Mum drove to James' house and knocked on their door but no one was there. I didn't think James would abandon me now that I needed him most. But in his defence, I thought that perhaps his father got scared because of what he mistakenly did to my mother and him and James fled town. I would have appreciated James guardianship into this unknown world.

Mum took control of things, I learned to control my emotions, it was a good thing that in the past I was not overly emotional. That helped me, especially now that I am armed with knowledge of what my anger could do if I let it loose. Mum was also dealing with her own emotions but she concentrated more on me. My mum owns a small bookstore; which had remained closed since my birthday. A few worried friends did come calling but she told them she was alright just taking time out to care for her son.

When it was the day, I was to return to school, Mum wouldn't let me go without sounding her final warnings into my ears.

"You have to be careful Harry Moon, you must not get angry, you must not scratch anyone at school be careful. When you think you are losing control Harry Moon just sing, hum the song I sing to you in your heart and it will calm you baby. You hear me?" I nodded. "That's my child, I trust that you will be fine. Just test it out, and if you don't think you can handle it. Just call me, I will come get you right away. Okay darling." I nodded again as she smoothed out my shirt. "You will be fine." She reassured but I felt like she was convincing herself more so than me. I smiled and nodded again. I was panicking inside but showing it would mean disaster. I shut my eyes and breathed out in stages. "Everything will be back to normal, if we want to be normal again, we must act normal," she continued.

I took a deep breath. I was scared about what returning to school might bring but my mum was right we had to act normal to be normal. "Okay mum," I finally spoke, doing my best to reassure her that I had everything under control.

We walked from the house together silently until I was outside the school gate. We both stared at the gate and the children rushing through the gate into the school compound. I looked at her, she looked at me, and I smiled and said.

"See you later Mum," she nodded; her eyes glistened with tears.

"See you later Harry Moon."
I walked through the gate not turning back until I was in my class.

# Chapter 5

## A Beautiful Girl

For the next three years, I maintained my pretence of being normal, no one got under my skin at school, and I made sure I never looked for anyone's trouble. I was more alert and I used that to my advantage at school. However, something strange was happening to me. As a wolf, I was growing in size but my human height grew at the normal human rate. I wasn't short but for some reason I became the butt of the joke in class. All my friends were taller than I was and it made me mad when they laughed at my expense.

When I got home from school, I couldn't sleep. I didn't want to talk to my mum about it and the anger remained until I shifted my form from human to wolf, I wasn't thinking. I stormed out into the night and went on a rampage. I didn't know what I was doing or what I had done but I woke up in my human form in the woods, an arrow buried deep in my left shoulder and a dead man lying on his side next to me. I was covered in blood and my body was in pain. I didn't know what I had done; I must have killed the man. Although I was in pain, I couldn't think beyond what I had done to the man. I screamed and then I heard a twig snap and a girl about my age, not older than 16, appeared from behind the trees. I noticed instantly how beautiful she looked; although I couldn't at that moment let it register because of the situation we were in. She stood looking at me shaking, she had a scarf round her neck, she pulled it closer to her neck as she looked on in dread and then she looked from me to the dead man on the floor and shouted.

"No! No! Father no!"
Afraid, my first thought was to run but I couldn't leave her after all I had done. I did this, I was responsible for her pain, and the monster that is the wolf took her father from her. She ran over to where we were, I didn't know what to say to her. I didn't know how long she had been standing there, if she saw me turn or not. She was confused and in pain and so was I.

"What happened!?" she yelled over her shoulder. "What did you do to my father!?" she continued to scream.

"I don't know, I don't know," I said,

"How can you not know, you were here?" she accused me.

"I promise I don't know what happened to him, I passed out and found this arrow in me, I don't know how I got here. Please believe me." Until then I hadn't realised, I was naked, that was when it sunk in for her as well.

"Where are your clothes, why are you naked?"

That I had an answer to but I couldn't very well tell her. "I…I don't… I don't know," I stammered.

She turned her father on his back and that was when we both realised, he had two sets of the same arrow embedded in his chest. I had never seen him before; I wondered what he was doing here with me.

"Someone must have been trying to kill him and I got in the way, or someone was trying to kill me and he got in the way." I quickly explained. She looked from the arrow in my shoulder to her father's

"That makes no sense to me at all. Did you know my father?"

"No, I never met him before now, here this morning." She closed his eyes, she looked up at me, I covered my naked self with my hands. "I see you got lucky then, whoever killed my father tried to kill you too," she accepted, then got up, untied her scarf and handed it to me.

"Take, cover yourself," she said and went back to her dead father's side. I heard her cry softly over him. "I'm on my own now father. You had to go and die, even though you promised you will never leave me."

"I'm sorry, is there anything I can do to help?" I interjected, ignoring the pain shooting through my shoulders.

She got up and looked blankly at me, "Can you wake him up, bring him back to life?" I shook my head from side to side. "Then no, you can't help me. I'm on my own now," she said again, tears rolled freely down her cheek. "I don't want to leave him here, but we need to get help," she said not looking at me. "We should call the police," she said, her eyes were so sad and I could not help blaming myself for her father's death. Perhaps if I had not come here, he might still be alive.

"If you don't mind, I think I should call my mum first."

She looked at me, and said, "I'm guessing you don't have a phone on you." I shrugged. "Okay I have one in our tent, come with me," she said and I followed.

We hiked about a half mile to her camp. Her and her father must have camped there overnight. There were two foldable chairs a fire that has been put out, a few things and a pickup van packed close by. She walked into the canopy she and her father must have slept in that night and brought out her mobile phone.

"Take, call your mum," she handed me the phone.

I quickly punched my mum's number in and dialled. The phone rang twice and my mum picked. "Mum, it's me, I'm in trouble," I said.

"Where are you, Harry?" Mum asked,

"I don't know, Mum. A man is dead. I woke up and found an arrow buried in my shoulder. I am scared, Mum, please come and get me." I said.

My mum was trying to be strong, but I could sense the fear in her voice. "Tell me where you are, I will be there at once."

"I don't know, Mum, I don't know…"

The girl snatched the phone from me and said something to my mum. I didn't hear what she said; I couldn't get past the panic I was feeling inside. I sat down and started to sing the song that calms me. The last thing I wanted to do was turn and hurt this girl. I sang the song over and over and over again. She came in front of me and said something but I wasn't listening to her, I had to sing the song so I don't harm her.

I don't know how long it took but I was still singing when my mum arrived. She walked over to me and knelt in front of me, she joined me in my song, and then I looked up at her. I smiled in relief and broke down in tears. My shoulder was hurting but it didn't matter at the time. My mother took me with her and we got to the car and opened the door. She placed me in the back seat of the car and returned later with the girl. She was saying something to her but I couldn't hear it. I felt awful, I had caused so much pain. Then I saw the girl get in the car with us. Mum sat behind the wheel; she placed a call to the police. I heard mum speaking on the phone, but I wasn't listening to what she was saying. The girl looked at me like I was a weirdo. She was in her own world of pain and I was in my own hell. Then mum drove us straight home. It must have taken about an hour before we got home; which meant I walked out of town as a wolf. I wondered how many more people I could have hurt along the way. This knowledge only brought me more guilt.

At home, my mum left the girl in the living room and took me to my room before she ran out to get bandages and antibiotics from the pharmacy. When she returned, she broke the arrow, and pulled it out. I yelled in pain, and nearly passed out as warm blood poured out.

Mum placed cotton wool over the wound and then immediately wrapped it in bandage. At first, we both thought I would bleed to death but then the blood stopped pouring out. Mum unwrapped the bandage and the miraculous had happened, the wound sealed. Mum looked at me in shock, we were both happy I was okay but we also knew that no one else could find this out especially as we had the girl with us in our house. Mum left a bandage on the wound so the girl does not suspect that the wound had healed.

The police came over to our house to speak to me and the girl. The detective asked her name, "Lana," she said and looked from the detective to me and repeated it again. "My name is Lana King."

Something happened within me at that moment. It was like I was seeing her again for the first time, clearer and more aware. For an instant our eyes locked. The detective cleared his voice, to get her attention; she looked away from me and refocused on him.

"Okay Lana, I will have to ask you a few questions so I can figure out what happened to your father." Lana nodded, her eyes watered, I looked away. "And Mrs Moon, um, if your son is feeling up to it, I will be questioning him as well. First, may I ask, you said he was stabbed in the shoulder with an arrow?"

My mum nodded, I looked up at her, as we both knew the wound had healed, there was no going to the hospital now and I had no more defence. "Yes, he got a really nasty gash, but luckily no artery was nicked. So, I was able to put a first aid bandage on it. I used to be a nurse in my old life." Mum lied, the policeman followed her with a nod of his head, as his eyes rested on mine. I winced a little to show pain. "He's obviously still very sore and when we are done here, I will definitely take him to the doctors to get him checked out," Mum lied again, as we both knew I had no wound to show any doctor.

"Okay, if you think he can handle it, I just want to ask them a few questions just to get a bearing on what happened out there; what they saw, if they did see anything and hopefully, we can figure out how Lana's father ended up dead." The detective then turned to me, "So, Harry, when I am done with Lana, I will ask you a few questions as well, if you are up for it; otherwise, you may have to come into the station to give a statement."

"It's okay, I can handle it, I want to help anyway I can," I said, my eyes back on Lana.

"Okay, that's great to know, obviously, your mum will be here as a legal guardian for you and she can step in for you as well Lana, and if there is anything too

difficult just let me know and we will stop."
Lana nodded. "Okay Harry, if you don't
mind may I speak to Lana on her own for
now? And mum, you can stay with her while
I question her if you don't mind."

My mum eyed Lana, "It's up to Lana
really if she wants me here. Let's ask her."
Mum said to the detective. "Do you mind if
I stick around while the detective questions
you?" she asked.

"It's okay, I don't mind. Thanks."
Lana responded.

"Great, then we shall begin. So, Harry
could you please leave the room for now," he
said turning to face me.

"Yes, absolutely, of course," I said as
I got up and faked a little wince as though, I
was still in pain. I went to my room, and laid
on my bed, and waited for my turn.

Fifteen minutes later, Mum poked her
head through my room. "He's ready for you
now Harry. How are you holding up?" Mum
asked in a whisper.

"How do you think? Mum, it's not
going to look good. I have no injury to show.
They will think I killed him," I voiced out
panicky.

"Hush, keep your voice down. You will be fine. Just tell him what you told me. You will be fine. I promise," Mum assured me.

"How can you be so sure mum? I'm scared."

Mum walked in and pulled me into her embrace, "Listen to me, she cupped my face in her hands, you are not a killer. You didn't hurt that man. I know you Harry Moon. You are my son. Now go out there and tell him exactly what you told me."

"I don't know what happened to her dad, I don't remember anything mum."

"I know, now go out there and tell him exactly that."

"Okay mum," I said and started walking into the sitting room.

I met Lana on her way to the kitchen, she stopped momentarily to look at me. I glanced back to look at her out the corner of my eyes, before going to meet the detective. I sat down trying to contain my nerves.

The detective cleared his throat. "This won't take long at all. I am just trying to get answers and I'm sure you will like to help us in any way you can," he said.

"Yes, I will," I said.

"Mum, you may join us if you like."

"Yes, um before you start, would you like a cup of tea or coffee?" Mum asked. I could tell she was nervous for me as well. I looked from her to the detective.

"No. I'm fine. This will not take long. Harry, just tell me what you remember, how you found yourself in the woods. Who attacked you? If you got a look at your attacker, you know things like that. How you know Lana's dad. If you've met him before last night in the woods."

I nodded, "Okay, um…" I looked from the detective to my mum. Mum smiled to encourage me. "Um, I just… I just woke up in pain. I don't remember much. I don't even remember leaving home last night. The last thing I remember was lying on my bed after dinner. Then, I… I woke up with a sharp pain shooting through my shoulder, but before I could figure out, what was happening, I saw the man, lying there…"

"Go on," the detective encouraged.

"I have never seen him before then, at first, I thought he was sleeping, then I saw the blood, which reminded me of the pain in my shoulder. I … I looked and saw that I had an arrow in my shoulder. I don't remember anything else, then… um… I saw Lana, she was looking for her father I guess."

"Then what happened?" the detective probed,

"Then, um… I was in as much shock as she was. Erm, Lana was in pieces over her father. I was trying to explain to her that I didn't know what happened to him and that I got hurt as well. Then, she turned him on his back and that's when… when we saw he had two arrows buried in his chest."

"Okay, you're doing great. So, tell me, what did you do after that?"

"Um, I didn't know what to do, I didn't know where I was, I… I… Knew I had to call my mum. That was all that was going through my mind, and of course; I knew that we had to call the police but we didn't have any… um… any phone on us. Um Lana, she said she had a phone in their tent, so we hiked until we got to the tent. We had to leave her dad there, there was nothing we could do for him. So, she gave me her phone and I called my mum, she came to us about an hour later and she called the police."

"Right, so you called your mum first, um is there any reason, your first call wasn't to the police straight away or even an ambulance? I mean, especially because you had sustained an injury. Why wait until an hour for your mum to come when you could have probably called for help and the ambulance would be there faster than, say, your mum."

"Yeah! I know what you're saying, but I wasn't thinking right. I was still in shock I will say. Cause I didn't know how I got there and then seeing the man dead, I was ... I don't know, I just wanted my mum I guess."

"Okay, I can understand that, but you know you could have still been in danger, whoever did this to you and Lana's dad could have still been around. Or, by not calling the ambulance, if Lana's dad was still alive at the time, which you couldn't have known, his life could have been saved."

"I don't think that it's fair to say that to him. You are trying to put blame on him. My Harry Moon used to sleepwalk a lot, I don't know how he got there, but if he says he doesn't remember, it must be because he was sleep walking. I thought that he had outgrown this problem, obviously, I was wrong. It has started again; there is no other explanation or any reasonable reason that explains why he was there. He is as much a victim as Lana's dad. He is lucky to be alive," Mum defended

"I know, Mrs Moon, I am just trying to establish the importance of calling the authorities to a crime scene. Lana's dad was pronounced dead, as soon as the paramedics got to the scene. Just so I know, tell me again, um until when you said you woke and saw him lying next to you, had you met or seen him anywhere before?"

I shook, my head, and tried to think but I knew that I had never seen him before. "No, no, not until I saw him lying there," I said, and watched as he jotted a few things down.

"Yeah, okay. So, what time do you say this all happened. Were you wearing a watch by any means?"

"No, I didn't. I didn't have anything on."

"Yeah, Lana mentioned that, apparently you were naked," he said as he looked up from his notepad. "How come?" he enquired.

"I don't know, all I can think of is that perhaps, I had gone to bed without my clothes. Just as Mum said, I have been known to sleepwalk at times other than that like I said, I don't remember anything. I… don't know what happened to him or who shot me with an arrow. I wish I could help more; I really can't remember anything," I said and grimaced, holding my bandaged shoulder gently and praying that this questioning would come to an end.

"Okay, I think that is it for now," he said.

I let out air in relief, conscious not to let him see me. I looked up and saw Lana by the entrance of the door. She looked at me, and I looked down. There was something about her, I couldn't place my hand on it. I knew she would soon leave with the detective and I may never see her again and the thought of never seeing her again broke my heart. A sharp pain pierced through me, and it wasn't because of anything other than the thought of never seeing her face again.

"Right, you and your mum, when you think you can make it, will have to come to the station to give an official statement. In the meantime, please make sure you see a proper doctor for that wound. You don't want it getting infected," he said, smiled and then got up. "Okay, I will have to take Lana with me. I will take her to her family," the detective said.

My mum nodded. Lana looked at me, I didn't want her to go and her eyes told me she wanted to stay but nothing was said between us. She walked into the room and joined the detective at the door. She turned around and looked at Mum and I before going to sit in the back seat of the detective's car. I walked to the window and stared from behind the curtains, her eyes were locked on mine as she was driven away.

# Chapter 6

## Lana's return

Two weeks passed since that unfortunate situation happened. My mum and I went to the police station a week ago to write down my statement. We were told we will hear from the police, if anything else happened. Then two days ago, the detective called to let her know that they were closing the case and ruling Lana's dad death as a hunting accident. That was a relief. To celebrate, mum ordered Chinese that evening and in the middle of dinner she announced that we had to leave. She wanted us to leave town, because she worried someone may have seen me change form; but we couldn't leave until the case had been closed. I wasn't shocked, I knew we would have to go soon. In fact, if I hadn't met Lana, I would have been overjoyed at the prospect of leaving this place and not coming back. Things had become difficult with my friends. I was tired of being poked on and having to walk away because I didn't want to hurt them or allow myself to get really angry. As sorry as I was to have been the reason, we were leaving town, this was a welcomed news. But then, Lana, why couldn't I forget her? Why did she haunt my dreams? I had no right, not after what had happened. Yet the more I thought that, the more my mind wouldn't let go. It was as though she crawled up in my head and made a home for herself. I wished I knew where she lived, so I could help her if she needed me, or just to see how she was doing.

As we ate dinner, my thoughts went to James; we were supposed to be brothers for life. That was not the case, he abandoned me when I needed him most. To think I once placed him on a high platform, now all I could think of is ripping his selfish head off his shoulders. Yes, I asked for it, but he could have stayed to show me the ropes, now I wish I had never set eyes on him. I was just someone to be toyed with. He didn't have to tell me about himself but he chose to target me. He knew I would want this and by so doing, destroyed my life just as his is. To think I was once the most popular kid in school, and now I'm the joke of the class. And how could his father leave my mum like that after he had scratched her, accident or no accident. As I thought about them, I felt my body getting warmer, my jaw clenching as anger began to build in me. I had to control it before things got out of hand.

"Let's start packing tonight," Mum said, pulling me from my thoughts. I nodded,

"Harry Moon, is everything alright?" she probed.

"I'm fine," I said, carelessly throwing down my chopsticks.

"You don't look fine to me Harry Moon. What is it, don't you want to go?""

"I said I was okay. I want to go, I was just… never mind. I'm fine, happy to leave," I said, showing her a false smile.

"Okay, if you are sure. I will go and get started in my room. Let's just take everything essential and leave the rest. I will sort those out later," Mum explained, as she cleared the table. I got up and walked away from the table.

Halfway out the dining area, I turned and asked, "So, where are we moving to, do you even know?"

"No, I'm still working on that. In the meantime, we have enough money to keep us afloat until I can find us a new home in a new city. We will have to do a lot of travelling before then. I need to find the ideal place with enough land to keep who we are hidden."

"Okay Mum, I trust you will find us the right place."

"No, we will do it together. We will both decide where we want to settle, okay?"

"Alright Mum, I'll get packing right away," I said and walked straight to my room. My heart was heavy, I knew we were doing the right thing moving, but that meant that if either Lana or James came looking for me in this home, I would be nowhere to be found. As I packed, my mind dwelled on all sort of things: where we would go, if I would like it there, would I be able to make new friends easily or will I be picked on and then forced to defend myself? I placed my game console into the box in my room. Everything was packed, aside from the bed I will sleep on tonight until we have to go. As I sat on the bed, thoughts of Lana came rushing in. I sniffed in air, and I could remember her smell. I regretted a lot of things the day I met her but what I regretted more was not doing more to talk to her. I stretched my body across the bed, placing my locked fingers behind my head and as I shut my eyes, I heard the doorbell ring. We weren't expecting anyone. I waited for my mum to answer it. The bell rang again insistently.

I forced myself up and walked to the entrance door in the living room. I peeped through the hole in the door, and saw the back of a girl, hair flowing down to her back. She didn't turn, I waited a while but she stood with her back to the door. I was curious, I paused for a moment and then I opened the door. As I did, she turned and it was her, Lana King. My heart stopped for a brief moment as I dumbfoundedly stared at her, and then as if by some magic, a strong wind blew her scent into me. I inhaled sharply, taking her all in and filling every part of me with her scent. My eyes closed and opened again, and my heart kicked back to life, beating in hard successions. She was still standing there, I continued to stare, she smiled. I should say something but I didn't know what to say to her. "Hello again, Harry Moon," she said. She looked pleased to see me; I was over the moon but I kept it hidden.

"Hello… Lana."

We were both quiet and then she asked, "May I come in?" I stepped out of the way and she walked in.

"What…what are you doing here?" I questioned.

She looked at me and shrugged her shoulders, and said, "I had nowhere else to go." She looked about her, "You don't mind that I came here, do you?"

"No! No, I don't mind at all." I said.

We continued to stare at each other awkwardly. I should say something else but what could I say when by some miracle the girl of my dreams that I never thought I would see again walks back in my life.

"Well this is awkward," she noted.

"Oh! I'm sorry, I should offer you something. Do you want a drink?"

"Yes, that would be nice," she smiled.

"Okay," I started to move to the kitchen, then I stopped.

"Um, Lana, it's nice to see you again," I said and she half smiled.

"It's nice to see you too," she said.

I felt joy that she had said that, I joined her and smiled softly, and I felt my heartbeat against my rib. This was no coincidence; something had definitely brought her back into my life.

I walked back with two cans of coke from the fridge, and handled her a can. She was still standing, she looked around as though she was looking for someone.

"Your mum, is she home?"

"Yes, she is um… in her room… packing?"

"Packing?"

"Um yes… we are moving, the day after tomorrow."

"Oh!"

"Yeah! I just found out tonight myself. If you had come here, say, two days later, we would have been gone."

"Why? I mean, if it's because of my father…"

"No, no… it's not that," I quickly interjected.

"You know they closed the case, apparently it was a hunting accident gone wrong," she said.

"Yeah, mum told me. How are you coping… I mean without your…without him?"

"I don't want to talk about that," she said

"Oh, sorry."

"It's okay," she said and looked from me to my mum who suddenly appeared.

"Who is this?" Mum asked and then she looked again. "Lana!" mum exclaimed and moved closer to where we sat. "What are you doing here?" she asked as she looked from Lana to me, confusion written all over her face.

Lana got up, "I know I shouldn't come here but, I was... I needed to get away and I couldn't think of anywhere else to go."

"Get away? Get away from what?"

"Mum, does it matter, she came here and I'm happy that she did."

"It's okay, it's only right I tell you this. Um, I had always been a foster kid since my grandmother died when I was five. My dad was never in the picture, he showed up once every three to four years. When we went camping, he had promised to never leave again. And then, he died," Lana explained.

Mum shrugged, she moved closer to give Lana a hug but Lana stepped back.

"I came here because, I had nowhere else to go."

"I thought the officer, said you had family."

"No, I don't. I don't even remember who my mum is. My dad said she left when I was a baby. She left me with my grandmother."

"I'm so sorry, you poor thing."

"I don't want pity; I just need a place to belong," she said and looked from me to my mum.

"I don't understand," Mum questioned.

"I want to come with you, if you will let me."

"Yeah, sure," I answered immediately.

"Wait a minute, we… we can't just… look, Lana, I know you've been through a lot. But we can't just take you with us. That's not how it works."

"Yes, we can," I retorted.

"Harry, common. She must have run from her current foster home. We can't be responsible for that. No offence Lana, I like you. I just wish the condition was different."

"Please, I beg you. Take me with you. Since I saw you two, that day, I have felt this weird connection, like… I don't know how to explain it… like, I'm meant to be here, to be a part of your family and I know that is saying much. But… please… I have no one else, I will pull my weight, I promise, I will not get in the way. Just take me with you."

"You won't be in the way Lana; you could never be in the way. I want you with us," I said. She smiled.

"Harry!"

"Mum, if you don't let her come with us, then I'm not leaving. I'm not going anywhere without her," I said firmly, trying not to get annoyed with my mum. I couldn't believe after all that has happened to Lana; she was willing to walk away from her.

"Alright…calm down. Let's talk about this tomorrow. I will get you a blanket Lana, you can sleep on the couch." Mum said.

"No, she can have my room. I will sleep on the couch."

Mum eyed me and sighed. "Alright have it your way. Lana, it looks like you will get Harry's room. I still have a lot of packing to do. I'll see you two in the morning." Mum began to walk away.

"Thank you… for letting me stay," Lana voiced out to her.

"Ah! Thank Harry," Mum responded and disappeared from view.

# Chapter 7

## Happy Times

That night, I couldn't sleep. Lana was here in my house, in my room, lying right now on my bed. A strange feeling consumed me all night. I tossed and I turned. Something magical was happening to me, I wanted to dance, shout, scream all at once. I knew she didn't know how I felt about her, I didn't understand it myself but she made me feel good inside and that was good for now. Morning came, I squinted my eyes as streams of sun ray bathed my face as I jumped up from my sleep. I had a good dream; I was getting married, there were white flowers on the floor, in a forest. My mother was there, and a few faces I don't recognise. My heart was beating fast as my bride to be moved closer. It was joyous, love at the purest. Only I couldn't see her face. She had a veil on, and then she reached my sid e and I was about to lift the veil up to reveal her beautiful face. I closed my eyes, and my lips formed her name, "Lana," I called out.

"Yes," she said as she sat next to my side. My eyes connected with hers now.

"Lana?" I asked confused.

"Yes Harry. You were calling for me in your sleep. Are you okay?" she asked as she gently placed her hand over my forehead to feel my temperature.

I realised now what I had done, "Oh!" I exclaimed as I tried sitting up. "Sorry, I was… I…never mind." I couldn't tell her I had the most wonderful dream of marrying her. If I told her that as much as it was a dream, I wanted that dream to come true, I am sure she would run for the hills.

"Your body is a little hot, do you feel ill?" she asked,

"I'm fine. I'm naturally hot-bodied. I think I got that from the family gene," I lied.

She giggled softly.

"I didn't thank you yesterday."

"What for?"

"For letting me stay. You haven't changed your mind, have you?"

"Oh no Lana. I haven't," I said. She smiled shyly.

"Anyway. Thank you. I appreciate it."

"Yeah, anytime," I said and we stared at each other for a moment too long. My heart began racing again, I looked away quickly afraid that she could hear it, and would know what I was feeling inside.

She looked down, and got up and said, "To thank you and your mum for letting me stay for the night, the least I can do is cook you breakfast. If you don't mind," She offered.

"Oh, that is very gracious, but you really don't have to do that," I said.

"But I insist," she said firmly.

"Oh! Alright then if you insist, then you must."

She smiled, "Would you like to come help me?"

"Oh, yes, of course. Let me show you where everything is."

"Thank you. So, tell me, what do you like?"

"I don't know, this and that. Anything you make, will be fine Lana," I said as I got out a frying pan, some eggs, oil, sausages, milk and flour and placed then on the working bench in the kitchen. Being so close to her was consuming me. Her scent was overpowering me and doing things to me, that I had never thought was possible. To think I had dreamt about marrying her and here she was, cooking me breakfast. I wondered how old she was.

"So, tell me this and you don't have to answer if I am being too intrusive," I said.

"Okay, what do you want to know?" she said, as she broke eggs into a bowl and began to whisk it."

"How old are you?"

"Oh! You're just gonna come out and ask a girl that?" she joked.

"Sorry, I did say you didn't have to answer," I said.

She placed the frying pan on the heat, and in a separate bowl she began mixing ingredients for a batter. I wondered what she was making, but my mind was not on the food. I could stare at her for eternity, she was that beautiful.

"Well, if you must know, I turned 17 yesterday," she said and poured the eggs in the pan.

"What! It was your birthday yesterday."

"Shock, yeah!"

"Oh well happy birthday Lana. I'm glad you're here now,"

"Thank you. So, your turn," Lana said as she stirred the eggs in the pot.

"What do you want to know?"

"How old are you?" she asked,

"Well you're older than me, by a week," I said.

"You mean it's your birthday soon. So, we are both 17," she smiled.

"No, technically, I am currently still sixteen," I corrected.

"Same difference."

"Yeah, old lady," I teased.

"Who are you calling old?" She took a handful of flour and threw it in my face. Lana clamped her hands on her mouth, giggling softly.

"Oh no! You didn't."

"I'm sorry," she said trying to stifle a laugh. But it was too late, I had cupped my own handful of flour and aimed it at her, Lana dodged and the flour hit my mum smack in the face.

"Oh! So sorry, Mum."

"Yeah, you should be," Mum said looking at the state of the kitchen.

"I'm sorry Mrs Moon. It was my fault. I started it," Lana jumped to my defence.

"I gathered that much. What is this?" Mum said referring to the cooking. Mum took a kitchen towel and wiped the flour off her face.

"Lana wanted to make us breakfast for letting her stay," I quickly explained.

"Oh, you shouldn't have, really. But thanks that is very thoughtful of you," Mum added.

"It's okay," Lana responded.

"I will clean up the mess, I promise," Lana quickly added.

"No, you don't have to do that, I will do that."

"Yeah, Let Harry help you," Mum said. "I will just lay the table."

Lana did the rest of the cooking in silence, though I was with her all through helping her with what she needed. We ate in silence and just as breakfast finished, Mum said, "Lana, first let me say… Thank you for doing this. It was delicious."

"You're welcome, Mrs Moon."

"And, I have had all night to think things through. I want to say, if you still want to come with us, you are more than welcome. I can see that you and Harry get along and that's what matters most to me. His happiness and yours of course."

"Really, I can come?" Lana said and jumped up to go hug my mum.

"It's okay. But you will need things and since you didn't come with anything, how about I give you some money so you can buy yourself the essential things you will need. When we settle down wherever we do, you can get a job, and buy more things that you will need. Of course, I will chip in here and there if you are ever cash strap. Just like I do for Harry Moon here."

"I don't know what to say, just thank you. Really, I appreciate you. The two of you are nothing but amazing."

"A little less of the amazing," I added.

"All the same, I'm really grateful," Lana remarked happily.

"It's okay. Let's just get ready; we leave tomorrow morning. All happy?"

I nodded, and so did Lana. I couldn't take my eyes off her, I loved that we could make her this happy and that I wouldn't have to say goodbye.

I don't know what this relationship will mean, are we going to be like brother and sister? That can't be, not when I have such strange strong feelings for her.

And what if she doesn't like me, the way I like her. I had not stopped to consider that. But none of that mattered now as long as I get to see her every day.

# Chapter 8

## Lana and I

We drove from city to city; it was nice to have someone other than my mum around. When she wasn't looking, I stared at her. I have caught her staring at me once or twice and then she giggles. I just wanted to make her happy, I loved her smile. To celebrate me turning 17, we went to fun parks and enjoyed a lot of rides together while mum looked on, she liked that Lana made me smile and for a while we both forgot about our secrets. It was good to have someone that was normal around that made us feel even more normal. One day, Lana and I left mum at the hotel and took a walk to the park. Lana jumped on a swing and demanded that I push her along. She laughed all the way through; the higher I pushed her the higher her giggles got. Knowing what she had been through, I was just so happy I could make her laugh. Then she screams, "Harry, stop now."

"I can't hear you," I pretended.

"Harry please my hands are weak. I feel like I'm going to fall," she protested.

"Okay, I will stop," as the swing descended, I held on tight, so she could get out.

As she got up, I stepped in front of her to hold her steady, but she fell into my arms instead. My heart skipped two beats, as I held her in my embrace.

"Are... are you okay?" I asked, not wanting her to leave my arms.

"I am now... but I will be even more when..." she let her words trail off.

"When what?" my throat dried as our eyes met, my heart raced within me and my breathing was uneven.

She leaned forward to kiss me, and my eyes closed and my lips parted. A warmth, like I had never felt, covered me as I felt her soft lips greet mine. It was gentle at first. I responded with a gentle kiss of my own. I didn't know what I was doing, but I knew I wanted more of what just happened between us for the rest of my life.

She pulled away and looked at me and said, "I have wanted to do that for a while now."

I didn't know what to say, I could not think of the perfect words to show her how I was feeling other than to show her by kissing her again. But before, that could happen, we felt a presence around.

I turned around to see who had disturbed this moment for us.

"Don't let me stop you, who needs cinema tickets when you've got real life love birds here," her accent sounded like she was a northern girl. She was holding an opened bag of cheese and onion crisp.

"Name is Evie by the way," she offered. Then four other boys approached us. "C'mon lads, we've got free show here," she said giggling, as she dipped her hands into her bag of crisp and crunched a handful into her mouth. "Yeah, go on, don't let us stop you," she teased. Her friends joined her.

"Sup," one of the guys said to her.

"Don't mind me, I was just watching these two love birds at it," she smiled again.

I could feel myself getting angry, I looked away from them and held Lana close. "Let's go," I whispered.

"Hey not so fast," Evie said standing in our way. "I haven't introduced my friends yet, this is Alex, Arro, Raymond, we call him Ray actually and Si, for Simon."

I looked them all over once, and nodded. "Okay, now, can you move out of our way. We need to get going," I said hoping they won't try to cause me problems.

Evie looked like she could do with a shower, her clothes were clean but filthy. Her other four friends weren't looking great either. I wondered when they last had a decent meal. I shook the thoughts from my head. Not that I didn't care, but my world was full now with Lana in it, and I didn't want to make room for new friends. Moreover, apart from Lana, making a new friend with James was what got me into this situation. I wish I had never met James; I wish he had never come to my town or to my school but he did and now I am a wolf. Evie stared at me and Lana. I tried to remain calm. The other four boys circled us, so that we were trapped between them. I hummed the song that calms me in my head as I could feel my blood boiling over with anger. "No please," I told myself, "Not here, not now. Not in front of Lana." I looked at Lana, she looked scared. To think we were having a beautiful moment a while ago and now all I can see on her face was fear.

"It's okay, don't be afraid," I said to Lana to calm her down. I stared at the boys keeping Lana close but making sure they knew if they picked a fight with me, I would always win.

"We are going to go now and you are going to step out of our way, or else," I said to Evie who narrowed her eyes as she placed a crisp in her month.

"Or else what?" she dared.

I laughed sarcastically, "You don't want to find out," I said firmly. "None of you do. Now if you please, kindly step out of our way." I made sure that Evie knew that she would regret it, I could tell she was still sizing me up. From her eyes, I could see she was thinking if I was really capable of taking down her and her friends.

"From where I stand, there is only one of you, not counting your missus there and five of us. How do you plan to take us down?"

I sighed, and stepped closer to her so she could see the anger brewing in my eyes. "You really want to test me?" I asked. I could tell I got to her, she stepped back and signalled to her boys to back away.

"C'mon boys, let's leave these losers to themselves. We have more important things to do anyway," Evie ordered. I held Lana close to me, and waited for them to leave. Lana threw her arms round me, this time it was out of relief.

I held her close, then whispered, "Let's get out of here before they come back."

Lana nodded and we quickly walked out of the park. I held the truth from mum, if I tell her, she would not let us go anywhere by ourselves anymore. But Mum could tell something was wrong, perhaps it was the wolf sixth sense, I don't know but she knew somehow.

"What happened?" she asked as soon as we got in.

"Nothing," I said. "We went to the park, had some fun, met a bunch of trouble- shooting teenagers on the way and now we are back." I said in passing not wanting to make a big deal out of it. Lana was still pretty shaken. I eyed her and she tried to look as normal as possible.

"Okay, if you say it was nothing then I believe you. But be careful in the future. We don't want no trouble or any unnecessary attention. You hear me the both of you?"

I nodded, made my way into the connecting room and kicked off my shoes and laid back on my bed.

I tried to push those misfits out of my mind. My eyes caught Lana's; she stood between the two rooms by the connecting door. I could tell she was relieved we were back safely. She smiled softly and I responded, my heart swelled just knowing she liked me too. I closed my eyes, and all I could think of, was the kiss we shared and how content she made me feel.

# Chapter 9

## Evie

## The Crew

Evie, always had her way with boys, bossing them about and making them do whatever pleases her. She was only about twelve, when she ran away from home. She had been wandering the streets now for about four years. Of the four boys in her crew, she's known Arro, the longest. They first met when Arro was about eleven. He had been placed in a home, which he ran away from and started sleeping rough on the streets. Evie didn't bother asking him what his story was, truth be told she was tired of hearing horror stories of what bad adults did to kids. If he left home, then there must be a good reason for him to have and that was good enough. They wandered the streets together, stealing what they could and learning every trick possible to survive. Then they met Alex. Alex had stolen some food from the supermarket and he was being chased by security. Evie and Arro hid him in a bin and sent the security man that came looking for him in the wrong direction. When the coast was clear, Alex who was about twelve at the time, came out and thanked them. He shared his spoils with his new mates and that was how a two-man band became three. For the longest time the three survived the streets together, having each other's back and doing whatever they deemed necessary to stay alive and evade the authorities. Going back into foster placement was not an option. Raymond and Simon joined Evie's crew six months ago; she was always on the hunt to find strays. The way she saw it, the more of them there were the easier it was to scavenge for more food. When Evie saw Lana and Harry at the park, her first hope was that they were runaways, which would have helped increase their circle. But things took another turn quickly, it may had been the way she had approached the situation, but she wasn't one to forgive such insolent bestowed upon her by Harry so easily. Evie was determined to make him pay when next they meet. It wasn't easy being a girl and the leader of the crew. She's had to make tough decisions to let the boys know that she was the one in control.

The way Harry acted, how he spoke with command, attracted her to him. Evie remembered the fire she saw brewing inside him, which only helped ignite her desire to have him be part of her crew. But for Harry to join, Lana had to go. Evie knew she couldn't have Lana in Harry's life if she wanted to be in control of him. There was something about him, something different that flamed her need to have him in her crew. Evie questioned herself, was it only because of the way he took control, or was she just being a girl that is attracted to a boy she doesn't even really know? He spoke down to her, like she didn't matter, and held on to precious Lana as though she was his universe. Yes, Lana was beautiful, anyone with eyes could see, Evie admitted; even though it pained her to admit this to herself. But in her defence, she only looks weathered because, it's been long since she's had a proper shower or slept on a decent bed, brushed her hair or even worn a beautiful dress like girls her age should be doing. Thinking about this fuelled her rage towards Lana. Evie knew she shouldn't be bothered about Lana, but she was; all the boys she's known had all wanted her attention, so why did Harry treat her like she wasn't worth anything. She once was the most beautiful girl in the room she thought, and if she had the same care as Lana did then she would feel beautiful again. As Evie stood in the middle of the abandoned warehouse, she and her crew called home, she stared at her own reflection through a broken mirror, and sighed quietly. Who was she kidding? Even if she had all the care in the world; she knew there was no competing with Lana's dark luxurious flowing hair, no competing with her smooth skin and rosy cheeks, her beautiful face. That angered her, she threw the mirror across the room, smashing it in the process. She wanted to know more about Harry And Lana, and find out why they acted like they were better than her, treating her worse than a piece of gum on their shoe heel. Then Evie decided that, although she maybe dirty, she wasn't going to allow Harry to treat her like one. That was why she had instructed Raymond to follow Harry and Lana undetected as they left the park.

She was still undecided, on what to do when next she crosses path with the two lovebirds.

Whether to teach them a lesson for making her and her friends feel like dirt or to incorporate them into her crew. Under Evie's command, Raymond followed Harry and Lana until they entered inside the hotel before returning to report his findings to Evie.

"I've seen them, enter the B&B," he said,

"Good lad," Evie said patting her solider on the back.

"First thing tomorrow morning you keep your eye on that B&B, if you sight them, tell me immediately and just follow them. We will get them, and teach them a lesson."

"You sure that's wise. What if they have an adult with them?" Arro interjected.

"Obviously if they are not alone, we abort, but if they are, we get them, nobody talks to us like shit. And he needs to pay, we need to teach respect," Evie affirmed.

"I don't know, something about him doesn't sit right with me. The way he looked at us, he was weird. I say we leave them alone," Alex said in his northern accent as he shook his head in disagreement.

Evie got up and walked circles round the boys, "I didn't know I was still dealing with boys, I thought you were lads, hard lads. Like it or not that's what these streets have taught us, made us into. We are more than what we look like, we are not scavengers, or just orphans tossed into the system. We are who we are, survivors. That's what these streets have taught us; how to survive, how to take down enemies, to ensure we remain untouched, on top always. You gonna let that boy scare you lot. If that's what you want, if you are too scared, then say so now. We abort. But if like me, you know who we are, and we are tough, unyielding, we take no crap from nobody, we take what is ours to survive, we seek out broken comrades like ourselves, damaged by bad adults and we give refuge, but as noble as that may sound, we will not be disrespected and that is where I draw the line. He disrespected us and it's up to us to let him know that he made a grave mistake. So, are you with me on this?" Evie asked looking from one face to the other. The four boys nodded in unison. "Great! That's more like it. Raymond, as I said before, you keep watch. Let us know. Simon, Arro and Alex, you will be with me. Once they come out, we lure them to the park, where we will handle this," Evie instructed.

They made ready the next morning to come to the Hotel, staying far enough so they can sight Harry and Lana when they come out.
Alex didn't like that they were spying on them. He didn't understand Evie's reason but he went along with it because he likes her a lot and she has looked out for the group; so, anything to make her happy, he would do. Besides, if he doesn't do as Evie asked, Evie always made sure he paid for his rebellion one way or the other. It was a way of keeping her boys in check, and everyone knew this, and no one wanted to invite her wrath.

# Chapter 10

## Love and Secrets

"Okay, you kids need to hurry up. We need to go quickly or we will be late," mum said.

"I'm ready." Lana declared.

"Okay, Harry Moon what about you?" Mum called.

"I'll meet you by the car downstairs," I replied.

"Okay hurry up darling. We mustn't be late. We really need to take a look at the house and decide if it's for us. The realtor said a couple already showed interest. Don't want us to miss out."

"Yeah Mum, I know it's important. I will be with you in a minute," I said.

I wasn't feeling well. All day I had been feeling like changing form. Like I wasn't in control of myself. I wished I could discuss it with mum, but since Lana joined our family, that had been a little difficult with all of us all cramped into two rooms.

While Lana and my mum left for the car, I splashed cold water on my face and inspected myself in the mirror.

"Get it together," I said. I knew I had to be honest with Lana; mum and I had to come clean and tell her what we really were. That could mean that we lose her forever, but I wasn't going to let something start between us with me hiding the truth. It was easier to think of telling her the truth than getting the courage to actually sacrifice what could happen between us.

I dried my face with the towel and headed downstairs to the car. Few feet from the car, I caught sight of one of the boys I had seen at the park the day before. It could be an entire coincidence, but what were the odds. I turned in the direction of the boy, but he had vanished. I shook my head, and wondered if I was seeing things, especially because of how I had been feeling all day.

Getting in the passenger seat, I strapped on my seatbelt and Mum brought the car to life. As Mum pulled out of the hotel carpark, I saw the boy again, on a bike at a distance. This wasn't coincidence I concluded but what could he want from myself or Lana.

I turned to look at Lana, she had not noticed anything. I decided I wasn't going to worry her or Mum until there was something to worry about.

Few minutes later, my Mum pulled into the driveway of a remote house we were to see.

As we got out of the car, the realtor was waiting for us. There was enough land around the house that we needed. And I didn't mind the house as long as it met Mum and Lana's needs.

"It's a four-bedroom house," I heard the realtor say as we walked in through the entrance door. "It's got two spacious entertaining rooms, a dining room leading from the kitchen," he continued to sell the house as he led us from one room to the other.

None of it mattered to me, I wanted this done with. I wanted mum and Lana to decide on a place. I was tired of sleeping in hotel rooms and travelling from city to city.

The realtor led the way as we made our way up the stairs to the rooms. He showed us three rooms, leaving the master bedroom for last.

Mum was in awe, so was Lana. I smiled to show participation. While they gushed and spoke about the cost of the house, I stared at

Lana. She looked happy. She was finally home with us. It would be a shame to ruin it all by telling her the truth but keeping the truth from her was just as bad. It was a struggle I didn't know how to deal with. I pretended as though I wanted to go look at the other rooms, Lana came to join me. I loved being alone with her but, not today. I was scared of hurting her. As I walked towards the window, she came towards me. I turned to look at her, we could both feel the energy between us as my heart raced the closer she got.

"What is wrong, Harry?" she questioned.

I looked away, "Nothing," I said.

"You've been off today, like you have something on your mind," she shrugged,

"It's nothing. I'm just a little tired" I lied and looked out the window.

Lana stood by my side, and I felt her hand reach out to hold mine. My heart stopped for a few seconds. I knew she could feel the heat radiating from my body.

"You're not well Harry. You're burning up," she said as her hands finally clasped around mine.

"I'm… fine," I struggled to say. I turned to face her. I could see that she was genuinely concerned.

"Look, I'm well… well not exactly… there is something… I need to…" I was about to tell her, but then through the window, a strong breeze blew in and with it was the scent of the boy I had seen outside the hotel. I looked out the window, and I saw the bike I had seen him on, by the tree.

I didn't want to alarm Lana, now I knew this wasn't coincidence anymore. He must have followed us here. But to what purpose, I thought.

As I was still processing the thoughts in my head, I heard Lana's voice cut through my thoughts.

"What were you about to say?" she probed.

"Um… it's nothing… really," I said. What was I thinking? I knew I had to tell her the truth but not now, and not here.

"No Harry, tell me. You know you can tell me anything right?" she pushed. Her eyes looked through me as though she could see the truth I was hiding. I felt helpless, I wanted to tell her everything.

"I… I am…" Mum and the realtor came to join us, interrupting my confession and saving my skin so to speak.

"So, what do you both think?" Mum asked, looking from my face to Lana's. Mum could tell I wasn't myself but she pretended she hadn't noticed anything. I was sure, she would be sitting me down for some heart to heart later.

"I really like this house," Lana voiced.

"I like it too," I said.

"Well, that makes three of us," Mum declared and turned to the realtor. "We will take it," she announced.

"Well then, I'll get on the phone to the owners and give them your offer. If they accept, then I think celebrations are in order," he said as he excused himself.

Mum was beaming with smiles as she took Lana, by the hand.

"Come with me, Let's go look at the kitchen again," Lana smiled and obliged, her eyes found mine as she left, letting me know that the conversation was not over. And mum gave me a warning look that said, what were you thinking?

Now that everyone was out of sight, it was time to find out what the boy wanted, that was if he was by himself. I hoped for their sake they were not coming to trouble us, or they may learn their lessons the hard way.

I went downstairs, and the bike had gone, meaning the boy was no longer lurking about. Whatever the reason he had followed us here, if this house became ours, I knew to be extra vigilant because Evie and her crew now knew where to find us. I would do anything to keep Lana safe from any harm.

# Chapter 11

## Lana's wrath

Three weeks later, we were moving into our new home. Mum and Lana were excited about the move. So was I, but I had other things weighing on my mind? Like the boy that followed us to the house when we first visited. The last thing I wanted was to hurt anyone, or to be angered to the point where I lose control and hurt them or even worse kill them.

The other thing was Lana. I had been trying to avoid her, it had not been easy though, as we live together. I am afraid of what I will say to her and how she will react. It wasn't just my truth to tell, it was my mum's as well and as long as my mum can pretend to be normal, I knew that I should try too for her sake. Mum had sold our formal house and sold her business too, so we had more money at our disposal as this new house was bigger than our last home.

Putting everything in my room, I sat on my bed, relieved to be finally out of the hotel. Lana's room was directly across from mine which meant we could sneak into each other's room without mum being any wiser. But I will not be doing that for now. It was best I kept my distance. I could tell that it disturbed her that I had kept my distance of late. I wish I could explain the real reason to her. I didn't want her thinking that I was no longer interested because that would be a lie. A month passed and we had settled into the mundane family routine. To help keep my feelings for Lana at bay, I decided to see her as my sister but that didn't work. So, I stopped doing all the things we did together, like going to help mum shop for groceries, walking to the park, going to the cinemas, swimming, helping her in the kitchen when she cooked, things like that; things that I had looked forward to doing with her in the past. Mum noticed my weird behaviour. It was not fair on Lana. I knew this but I was convinced that I was keeping her safe and making sure she had a home and a family.

After another awkward dinner, mum visited me in my room.

"Okay Harry Moon, talk to me," she said as she sat on the edge of my bed.

"About?"

"You know, Lana. I saw her face earlier. It looked like she's been crying. What happened between the two of you? You used to love to hang out together what changed?" Mum queried.

I felt bad; I was causing the girl I love pain. Wow! I love her, I guess I always knew that. I looked at mum.

"I don't know what to do, I feel like we are lying to her." I whispered.

"Lying to her about what?"

"You know, what we are."

"Oh! That. Harry Moon, we will cross that bridge if we ever need to. She doesn't need to know and what she doesn't know won't hurt her," Mum explained.

"Yeah, but as long as we all live together, she needs to know the truth. And that's why I have been avoiding her. I can't bare lying to her face."

"But we are not lying, we are just not telling her," Mum argued.

"Same difference, not telling someone that we care about that she is living with wolves is not cool," I retorted.

"Hey! Keep your voice down. She's only across from you," Mum said.

"I don't know what to do, I want to tell her but it's not just my secret. I think we need to tell her together."

"No! I forbid it. I won't let this thing dictate my life. If you tell her and she runs away, who knows how many more people she will tell? Our cover will be blown. We only just got here and I don't intend to run again with my tail between my legs. Do you understand me Harry Moon? Under no circumstances must you divulge this to Lana."

I sighed, mum was right, but so was my argument to keep Lana in the loop. Especially if I don't want to lose her altogether.

"I don't know what to do then? I don't know how to be around her knowing I am lying to her."

"Well you better find a way. You were doing fine before; you were okay going everywhere with her before, what changed?" Mum questioned.

I looked from my mum to the door, I wondered what Lana was doing at this very moment. I didn't know if I should share my feelings for Lana with mum. I wasn't sure if she would be against it or encourage me to be with Lana. Not that I can now, since I have been forbidden to ever tell her our secret.

"Nothing, it's just the guilt. It is eating at me," I explained.

"Well get over it, how do you think she feels. We, at your insistence have given her a home. Don't ruin it for her. We are a family now, you, Lana and myself. Now go to her and apologise for your behaviour. Make it better, make her feel better about being here," Mum said.

"Okay, I will," I said.

"That's my boy. I'm going to bed early. Don't disappoint me again," Mum warned as she exited my room.


I waited a few minutes after mum's departure, before going to knock on Lana's door. I tried rehearsing my apology. But nothing I made up in my head felt like an acceptable apology.

My head was facing down, as I knocked on her door for the third time.

"Lana please, may I come in?" I asked.

The door opened slowly; she was already in her nightwear. As I looked up, her beauty blew me away. I forgot what I came to say to her as I stared at her. Reminding myself it was rude, I quickly looked away.

"What do you want Harry?"

I opened my mouth, but words didn't form. I took two quick breaths to still my heart before trying again.

"Can we… talk?" I asked, doing my best not to look past her eyes, which were themselves mesmerizing.

"About what? Wait let me help you, is this talk going to be about how you've changed, how you pretend that I don't exit. You never look at me, you don't want to be around me and I get it. We kissed once and you realised, I'm not it for you, but you feel like you are stuck with me in the same house and can't escape. So, you treat me like dirt instead. Thought we were special, I was so wrong, I was…" she said in anger.

I wanted to stop her; she couldn't be farther from the truth.

"No, No! That's not true," I said cutting her off.

I shook my head from side to side as her words cut through me. I wish, I could tell her the truth. I was truly between a rock and a hard place as they say. I couldn't betray my mum or disobey her.

"No? Then tell me why. I'm a big girl, I can handle you telling me you are not interested. And I will try to get over you, I mean, it will not be so easy because I have no choice but to see your face every day. But do not lie to me. I don't want you to spew me lies to make me feel better," she paused for air, before she could continue, I quickly interjected.

"I don't want to lie to you, never."

"So, why then? Is it because you don't feel like I do?" My eyes layered with water, I fought to keep them away as I watched tears stream down her cheek. "C'mon tell me, I can handle it," she pushed.

"It's not why," I said as my right hand moved off its own accord to wipe the tears off her face. She took a step back and my hand dropped back to my side.

"So, you feel something for me?" she asked.

I sighed, biting my lower lips, I nodded.

"No say it, tell me what you feel for me," she continued to push.

"Lana, let's not… let's not do this."

"Let's not do what, let's not be honest?"

"No, I don't mean that, I just, you know how I feel. You've always known," I said.

"No, I don't, I thought I had an incline but of late, I see that I've been wrong. You've acted like I don't matter, like you want me gone. Is that what you want. I will go back to the streets if it's what you need to be yourself again," she said raising her voice.

I looked down; this was more difficult than I had thought it would be. "No Lana, I don't want that," I said raising my eyes to hers.

"Then what do you want Harry?"

"I want you to be happy, I want you to feel loved," I said taking a step closer to her. I could hear her breathing get heavier the closer I got.

"Then tell me the truth Harry, what do you feel for me?"

"Lana, I …lo…" I couldn't bring myself to say the words. Telling her I love her meant I couldn't hide the truth from her. I was overwhelmed by my emotions but I knew I couldn't tell her the truth, and if I couldn't, I didn't think I had a right to ask for her heart in return for my lies. So instead of the truth, I said, "I love… the way we were before, and I'm sorry about the way… I've been these past weeks. I care about you. You must know that, and I will do better from now on. You're… important to me."

She looked away; I could read the disappointment on her face. She had expected me to declare my love for her, and I didn't.

"I get it now, I am important to you, like a sister is to a brother." She smiled sadly, "I get your message Harry, loud and clear. I will carry on as normal. I will push these feelings I have for you away. I mean, who needs them, they are just a burden after all. The pain, the ache, the heart break, it's not worth it. So, if that's all you came to say. I understand better now. You may leave, and let me get back to my life."

I was responsible for her pain, and I was in hell myself. Hearing her say she will get over her feelings for me killed me. I wanted to be with her, I wanted to tell her, that I had changed my mind. She turned away, and the moment passed.

I tried to think of something to say, but nothing came to mind. My world felt like it had fallen apart as I turned away and walked into my room. I was sinking, drowning in sorrow. Why was I doing this to myself, why couldn't I just keep my secret and still have Lana? Like mum said, what she doesn't know couldn't harm her. I got up and walked to my door and for some reason, I couldn't summon the courage to rap on her door again. Feeling defeated, I coiled on my bed, and wished that I could redo everything again. I knew then as sleep finally claimed my body, that I had lost the girl of my dreams.

# Chapter 12

## Mum's fury

Three weeks passed; things didn't exactly return to normal. Lana and I were cordial in front of mum but if we ever found ourselves alone, we never spoke.

I couldn't give her what she wanted and she wasn't going to be with me unless I could tell her the truth. I watched out for the family in ways that I knew how. I didn't think there was a need to let mum in on what happened with Evie and her gang, especially because, I had not informed her that we were followed. Each time Lana went out on her own, I secretly followed her keeping a healthy distance just so she didn't see me. It was on one of these walks when I saw first-hand how sad she was. I had never seen her so unhappy. She sat on a swing close to the woods that surrounded our land and wept. I wasn't sure what made her so unhappy, could it be because she was missing her father, or because of how we've both been around each other recently.

I knew I had to fix it. I couldn't let this carry on. I had to tell her. I wanted to be with her and offer to tell her the truth. That will really anger my mum, but I couldn't have Lana's unhappiness on my conscience.

I waited for her to get herself together, she was taking her time. I hoped she wasn't deciding that she had had enough of us as a family and would like to leave. As I contemplated what to do for the better, I saw a shadow from the woods, hovering above her. I wanted to call out her name just to warn her to watch out for herself but I wasn't sure what or who I saw. I moved a little closer, and the shadow I had seen was that of a wolf, a black wolf. This wasn't going to happen on my watch. Lana wasn't going to get killed while I looked on helplessly.

I thought if I could get to her on time, we could run for safety before any harm was done, but as I ran towards Lana. I saw the shadow become two. There was another wolf, a grey one, and they both flanked her on both sides.

"Lana!" I called.

She looked up; her face etched with confusion. I didn't want her to see that her life was in danger. However, it was too late, the wolves came into full view now. Lana got up quickly as she noticed the danger she was in.

"Harry! Help!" she cried. One of them turned its head in my direction and the other moved slowly towards, her. I had no choice, I wished I had told her, I wished what I was about to do wasn't going to scare her more and see her running for the hills but it had to be done if I wanted her safe. As the grey coloured wolf turned towards me, I leapt into the air and changed my form. Pouncing on the grey wolf and pushing it to the side. There was no time to fight, I just needed to get to Lana first. I didn't have time to see her reaction to my transformation. Moving quickly, I leapt up again, I could hear screaming and I knew it was coming from Lana, but not because she was hurt it was out of fear. Lana began to run and the black wolf, ran after her. I leapt up again and landed my paws on its back stopping it in its stride. I felt the grey wolf on my back but anyone with eyes could see that I was far bigger than the two of them combined. I don't know how, but with the strength of my jaw, I lifted the black wolf into the air, and flung it away from me. I must have torn off part of its flesh as I could taste its blood in my mouth. From the corner of my eye, I could tell I had hurt it, it whimpered in agony. This must have angered the grey wolf as it dug its fang into the skin of my back, I tumbled to the ground and managed to get her off me. Before I could make it back up, her fangs burrowed into my legs as though she wanted to start tearing out my flesh. Twisting around in circles, I kicked her in her neck. She whimpered loudly and I quickly got up. She clearly got me, as I could feel pain shooting up my leg. But I wasn't going to let her see that I was hurt. Growling, I bare my teeth out, and crouched to attack. She ran towards me, leaping half her body into the air. I waited until she was close enough before leaping into the air gripping her neck in my jaw. One bite and she would be dead, she knew it and I knew it too. It felt like the right thing to do. Kill her off and then go and finish off the black wolf. That way, I was sure I would not have to look over my shoulders again and Lana would be safe. But I couldn't bring myself to do it. I was not a killer, even though the animal instinct in me was convinced I was making the right decision. I flung her to the side. She landed with a loud whimper but I wasn't done. Even though I was sparing their lives, they needed to know that I was not going to allow such attacks around my home in the future. I moved my head closer to her face. She got up halfway and bowed her head in defeat. Blaring out a loud growl to warn her off, she took off and I saw the black wolf join her as they both disappeared into the woods.

The easy part was done, but I was sure Lana had seen me earlier as I ran to save her life. That was the hard part. How do I explain any of these to her without her kicking off? That is even if she has not already packed her things and left.

Looking around to see if there were any other witnesses, I walked towards the house, and then changed back to my human form. Mum must already feel that something happened, the details I can explain later. First thing's first. I got into the shower to wash off the taste of blood and the scents of the wolf from my body. As the water glided over my body, I watched as the wound I incurred in the fight begin to heal. The flesh came together and my skin healed like it never took place. I wonder if it was so for every wolf. I had not seen my mum heal yet, maybe it was because, she had never cut herself accidentally or on purpose. Mum was always too careful, ever since she saw my body heal. She doesn't want any kind of attention drawn towards her or towards me.

Dressing in a top and a pair of shorts, I took sharp breaths as I headed for Lana's room. I hesitated a little before rapping on her door.

"Lana," I called. There was no response. "Lana please let me in," I pleaded. Although it was silent, I knew she was in there. I could smell her from where I was but most importantly, I could smell her fear. I closed my eyes regrettably. This was the last thing I wanted, but the cat, as they say, was out of the bag now and I just had to find a way to manage this crisis.

"Please Lana, let me explain. I know you are in there. Don't be scared. I will never hurt you."

"Go away please."

"Lana, I just need a minute, just give me a minute to explain everything."

"Please. Just leave, please," her voice was shaky. I clearly wasn't making anything better.

I turned, and at the end of the hallway, stood my mum.

Her eyes told me everything I needed to know. I was in trouble with her. Breathing deeply.

"Okay, I'm going to leave now, Lana. But please understand that I will never hurt you. What you saw, only happened because I needed to protect you," I waited for her to say something but she was quiet again. "Okay, I'll go, I'll give you your space," I said and walked towards my mum.

"My room now!" Mum commanded.

Mum locked the door behind her, her eyes were fuming. Before she said anything, I put my hands up to explain.

"Mum, I had no choice."

She shook her head in disagreement. "No, I don't buy that Harry Moon. You had a choice."

"I really didn't, if I didn't do something Lana could have died."

"What!?" Mum exclaimed.

"There were two wolves at the park behind the house. I don't know if they just happened to be there and it was a case of wrong place wrong time or if they came there on purpose."

"Slow down, I don't understand you."

"I went looking for Lana and I saw two wolves circling her. They would have killed her. I was running to save her and my instinct kicked in and I changed. And I think Lana saw me."

Mum's eyes widened, "Are you sure?"

I nodded, "I'm sure, she's scared of me now."

"Is that why you were knocking at her door?"

I nodded.

"I need to go speak to her; she needs to understand that I will never hurt her. She means so much to me."

Mum was quiet, I could tell I had made things worse for her. I promised her I wasn't going to tell Lana but instead I showed Lana. "I'm clearly not happy that this has happened. We will both have to speak to her together. If she decides to run, or doesn't want to live here with us anymore, I really don't know what we will do. I mean, she will leave us no choice."

"What do you mean by leave us no choice. We are not going to hurt her," I warned.

"No! Of course not! What do you take me for, I mean, if she leaves, who knows who she will tell? Then we are no longer safe. We will have to sell up and move again."

"Oh! Okay, I don't want her to leave. She has no one else. I won't see her put out with no one."

"That clearly isn't our decision to make, it's up to Lana now what she wants to do. We can't force her to stay but be prepared if she goes, we have to leave too, I can't risk your safety. Also, who knows who those two wolves were. They probably live close and were marking their territory. Something tells me we haven't seen the last of them."

"I'm sorry, mum. I know you didn't want this and now, I brought trouble to us," I said apologetically.

"Don't worry about it, as you explained, you didn't have a choice. Now, let's go talk to Lana."

# Chapter 13

## Fear

"Lana please open the door darling. I need to speak with you," Mum said, and I hung back behind her.

My heart was racing, I didn't know how this conversation was going to go or how long we were going to stand outside her door for until she lets us in. Suddenly, I saw the door crack open, relief washed over me as Mum glanced at me and gestured to me to follow her.

Lana was sitting with her back to the wall, her face looking down and a packed bag on the floor beside her.

"I see you've clearly decided you are leaving us," Mum said softly. Lana didn't respond. "I can't deny what you saw, so I am not going to come in here and lie to you. Harry can change into a wolf," Mum paused for a moment, before adding, "and so, can I." With that Lana's eyes darted upwards.

"Look don't be scared; we care about you. You've been living with us for so long now and we have shown you nothing but love. You are one of us, you should already know that by now. Harry did what he had to do to protect you. You were in danger and he had no choice but to change, because in his human form, he clearly didn't have a chance against two wolves. He did that, even after I forbade him not to tell anyone about this. Look, I can't force you to stay if you don't feel safe around us anymore but if you have already made up your mind to leave, go knowing that we love you and we hope that you love us as much and won't tell anyone what you saw," Mum said.

Lana looked up, "I'm sorry. I want to understand,  but I guess, the fear of what I saw ate me up inside. Looking at the two of you now, I feel stupid packing my bag. I know you will never hurt me. I just need to get my head around it, if you don't mind. I need some time to get used to the idea that you are both wolves."

Mum laughed softly. "Well if you put it like that, but we were first humans. Maybe one day I can tell you how this all began," Mum said.

I looked on, I saw that even though she was comfortable speaking to my mum, she hardly looked in my direction. Maybe it's because it was me she saw turn into the wolf and not Mum. But I was happy she was coming around to the idea and not running for the hills. I let myself breathe again. I wasn't aware how long I had held my breath for.

"Okay, for now we will give you your space. I made dinner already. If you don't feel up to eating with us yet. I understand, I will put a plate out by your door," Mum gently reached out her hand and caressed Lana's hair softly before getting up. Lana smiled softly; her eyes met mine briefly before looking away. I walked out of her room and heard mum say, "Do you need a hand unpacking that bag?"

Lana laughed softly. "No, thanks, I've got it," Lana responded.

"Well then, I'll take my leave now."

Outside Lana's room, mum smiled with content. I could tell she was glad that went well, maybe too well, I thought. What if Lana was just agreeing so she could run off later. I was clearly reading too much into things.

"I think I will skip dinner," I told my mum.

"Oh! Why?"

"Nothing, just don't have appetite for food now,"

"Okay, I will make you a plate and keep it warm in the oven should you feel like it later," Mum said and left for the kitchen.

I looked back towards Lana's room and wished I had told her about this before all of this took place. There was not much I could do now, so I went into my room, and laid on the bed. My mind wandered to the fight, and then back to Lana and then to Evie and her little friends and I was sure something big was going to kick off soon.

It was all too much for my head to take, I couldn't let myself worry about things I had no power over and before I knew it, my body switched off into unconsciousness out of exhaustion.

# Chapter 14

## Lana's disappearance

I felt the ray of sun beaming down on my face. I swallowed and licked my lips. I had dreamt of Lana, what exactly took place in the dream was fading with each moment I became conscious. But I was happy, the dream made me happy and, in that moment, I realised what had happened the day before. I finally opened my eyes, and pulled myself to a sitting position. I want to go and check on Lana right away but at the same time I knew she needed the space and with time, if she felt the need to ask any questions then I will tell her the truth. It was great to finally feel like a weight had been lifted off my shoulders. Maybe now she will understand why I became distant with her and if she is open to it, perhaps we might even begin our relationship again. The thought of kissing her again made me happy but if I was being honest with myself, I knew the chances of that happening were very slim at best. I can't imagine her kissing me without thinking of the wolf. Forcing myself to my feet, I walked into the shower room and washed, changing into something very comfortable, I walked towards my door. Only to be greeted by my mum.

"Good you are dressed; you have to start packing now," Mum said, her voice was panicking. I didn't understand why the change of heart. I thought we had smoothed things over with Lana the night before.

"Packing! But why, I… I thought…"

"Well you thought wrong, Lana has left," Mum said. At that moment, the thought of never seeing her again made me feel so faint.

"She can't be, you heard her yesterday, she decided to stay."

"Well she fooled us both. She clearly didn't feel safe because all her things are gone. I just popped my head into her room to see how she was and I saw a note on her bed saying *sorry*. So now we must leave. She clearly can't be trusted now to keep our secrets."

"No Mum, I don't believe it, she won't just leave!" I said walking swiftly pass mum and into Lana's room.

My two hands went up to the sides of my face. I couldn't believe that it was true.

"She's truly gone," I felt my mouth say.

I blamed myself for sleeping like a dead dog. If I hadn't allowed the sleep to consume me that much maybe I could have talked her into staying.

Mum walked in after me, "See for yourself, she's gone. And we have to go now."

"No, she won't tell anyone mum. She must have been too scared and maybe needs time to process it all. If we go now, we will never be able to see her again. What if she comes back?" I argued.

"Well what if she doesn't. I mean at this point after all I have done for that girl, I don't think I have it in me to take her back," Mum said. She was clearly very upset and so was I but my focus was mainly to do with worry for Lana and her being on her own.

"Well mum I still don't want to leave, not yet anyway. I didn't like it when we slept in hotels, I like it here," I protested.

Mum sighed, "I don't want us to take the risk Harry Moon. This is our lives you are putting in Lana's hands. I mean after the deception into making us believe that she will stay, I can't trust her again," Mum argued.

"I know you don't Mum and you may be right in your thinking but my gut feelings tell me, she will be back. And when she does come back, I want to be here for her." I insisted.

There was silence in the room, Mum could tell that it was pointless arguing with me over Lana. I wasn't going to move on this. I was sure that mum had an incline that I liked her, she just doesn't know by how much I adored Lana.

"Okay, we will stay a while, not more than three days. If she doesn't come back by then, I don't care what you say, we are leaving."

I nodded. "Okay, thanks Mum." I let out air in relief.

My instincts were to go out and find her. I knew her scents very well, I could track her down before she got herself and us in trouble.

I hoped that once I did, she would come back with me and not be fearful of us.

"I'm going to eat breakfast; do you want to join me?" Mum asked.

I was hungry but eating was the last thing on my mind. "No mum, I need to go and track her," I blurted out. I had wanted to hide it from her but there was no point in keeping secrets. If Lana was going to tell our secrets, it would not be only me that it would affect.

"Do you think that is wise? She clearly left cause she is fearful of us," Mum tried to make me see sense, but my mind was made up.

"I have to try, it's the least I can do. If I stay home, I will only worry constantly," I told her.

Mum shook her head in hesitation. "I don't know if that is clever but I see you've made up your mind. Surely Lana must mean a whole lot to you. But Harry Moon, if you must go, then I won't stop you, just promise me that you will be very careful. I don't trust her now, and I don't want her accusing you of things in public. People are not kind or understanding of what they don't know," Mum said.

"I will be careful. If I see her, I will only approach her when she's alone," I assured Mum.

"Very good, make sure you're home before dinner, I don't want to have to worry about tracking you down," Mum said as she lifted my chin with her hand, concern etched all over her face.

"Don't worry Mum, I will be back before you know it."

Quickly, I put on my shoes and her hat and breathing in Lana's scents, I began my search.

# Chapter 15

## The Fight

As I stepped outside the front door, I noticed the bike from Evie's gang a few yards from our house. My worry about Lana's safety increased. I half jogged over to the bike, and looked around but there was no one there, it looked like the bike had been abandoned. But what worried me most was that I could smell Lana's scent mixed with other unknown scents.

Tracking the scent, I found myself walking towards the field where I had fought off those other two wolves. My heart began to race within me, I could feel Lana's fear from where I was. Through the open field just before getting to the woods, I noticed a bag, it looked like the same bag Lana had used to pack her things the night before. I ran towards the bag and opened it to find that all of Lana's belongings were in the bag but she was nowhere to be found.

Just then, another scent greeted my nose. This one was familiar, and it felt close. I turned to find Evie behind me with a pocketknife pointed at me.

"Hey freak!" she voiced. She looked shaken but I could tell she was trying to put up a front for me.

"What are you doing here? And what have you done with Lana?" I questioned, dismissing the knife she pointed in my direction.

"Hey look here freak, I'm the one with the power the last time I checked. Unless you want me to hurt you, you will tell me where those other two freaks like you took my friends," she said.

I was shocked. "What are you talking about? And why are you calling me a freak?"

"Don't act surprised, I know what you are, I saw you change the other day. Yeah! That's right, I saw the whole thing with my two eyes and if you think of any funny ideas about hurting me, I have made sure that if anything happens to me the whole world will know that you are a freak. That's it, now turn around and take me to the rest of yous."

I felt my heart skip a beat, I was fuming, not only were we exposed to Lana, now Evie claimed she knew what we were. I could deny it but from the look on her face I would only be fooling myself. I could play along or I could turn this around and threaten her instead but my concerns at this moment were only for Lana. And if she had seen what happened then she was of more use to me alive and not afraid.

"Okay listen, Evie, I don't know what you think you saw, or what you were on that is making you see things that are not there, but know this, Lana is missing and so are your friends. At this point, I suggest we work together to find them. So put that knife away, and I will help you any way I can or you can keep pointing that thing at me and see how far you will get with finding your friends," I said and turned towards the woods.

I now knew that Lana must have been taken by the two wolves or other wolves from their pack.

"Just so you know, I'm not afraid of you," Evie said.

Without turning to look at her, I said, "Good, I don't want you to be. But put that thing away now, I hate feeling threatened."

Picking an item of clothing from Lana's bag, I began walking towards the woods.

"Where are you going? Evie called.

"To find Lana," I replied.

"Then I'm coming with you," she said walking
briskly to catch up to me.

"Your choice really, but know that you could be putting your life in danger by doing so. I am going to find Lana; you and your friends are no concern of mine," I voiced.

"Oh! I thought we were working together, isn't that what you suggested," Evie shouted, throwing her hands in the air.

"Yes, but now I change my mind as it occurs to me that you and your pathetic friends didn't have any business being here. You don't live around here but yet here you are. You must have meant to do Lana harm. So why would I help any of you?"

"Well what if I don't give you a choice, remember, I know things," Evie bluffed.

"Well, I think if you really are sure of what you claim to have seen, you won't be foolish enough to threaten me now. Hence why you and your minions are on your own on this one. You are free to follow me if you want. But make no mistake, I will do all that is possible to keep Lana and my family safe and if that means shutting you up for good, I won't think twice about it. Personally, I don't take to blackmailers," I said and walked into the woods leaving her rooted on the spot.

Then I heard her run towards me, "Hey, who said I saw anything. I was just being mouthy back there. You know when you've lived like I have to; you have to be willing to do or say anything to protect yourself. I just want my friends home, same as you want your Lana. Please help me."

I stopped and thought about it, her eyes looked genuine. "And of what you claimed to have seen, will you be spreading your rumours?"

"No, I didn't see anything and there's no rumour to spread."

"Okay, I'm not promising anything. I don't know what I will find and how many there are but I will do my best to see that Lana and your friends are safe," I assured her and we both continued to walk in silence.

After walking for about half an hour, the woods became thicker, and a weird darkness loomed over us. I could feel Evie's fear although she did not voice it, I could hear her heart racing inside her. We were too far deep for her to return to safety and I wasn't going to abandon my search now when Lana's scent was getting ever so close. I wanted to ask Evie if she was alright but I already knew the answer to my question so I kept my mouth close. Ten minutes later, we arrived at a clearing and from a distance I saw what looked like a small cabin. I knew I   f they were hiding Lana in the woods; we had just come upon the place. It could be a trap to draw me out, I thought, because I couldn't think of what anyone will want with Lana.

I turned to Evie, "Stay here, whatever you hear don't come out do you hear me?"

She nodded emphatically, "But what if you need help, I can help you."

"No, I don't want to add you to the list of those I need to protect. Just stay here. Once I free your friends, I will send them to you and you can all go and never come back again because if I think you are a threat to me and mine, you won't like the other me that you claimed to have seen."

Evie, nodded, "Like I said earlier, I didn't see anything."

"Okay, good. Hand over that knife and just wait here for me," I commanded and took the pocketknife from her.

Walking about two yards around the edge of the woods, to the back of the cabin. I saw Evie's four friends tied to the back of the tree with gags around their mouths. I didn't see Lana but I could smell her, her scents were mixed up with other stronger scents that I figured belonged to the wolves that took her. First thing's first I thought, free the boys, but I also knew that if I could smell the wolves, they probably can smell me too.

Walking swiftly to the boys I took out the knife and cut them free. Leaving the gags on their mouths, I gestured to them to follow me. I walked them back to where Evie was, it wasn't until then that I noticed they had been battered. They were all looking black and blue. I didn't feel sorry for them as I was sure they must have first taken Lana to harm her before the wolves got hold of them.

I took out one of their gags, and asked about Lana's whereabouts. "Where is Lana?" I asked.

"They took her inside with them," he said.

I nodded and mouthed thanks. Looking at Evie, I said, "Now you all have to get out of here, I'm going back for Lana."

"But we can help," Evie said.

"No, look at the state of your friends, they look like they need a doctor. Now get out of here before it gets too dark for you to make it out. I will be fine," I assured.

Evie held my hand and smiled, "Thank you." I nodded. Then she turned to her friends, "Let's go quickly," she said.

I didn't wait to see them go, I walked back but this time around, there was no hiding, they were waiting for me. A woman and a girl about Lana's age and looked like she could very well be Lana's sibling and a man.

"We knew you would come for her." the woman said,

I looked at them all, I could tell the girl was the one I fought the other night with the way she sneered at me.

"You took my friend. I want her back," I said with authority. In my head I had calculated that if I could fight two of them, then another one added into the midst wouldn't be too much of a problem.

"Well she's ours now, and if you want her, you will have to fight us all to get her," the woman said sternly.

"I don't like the odds but I guess if that is what it's going to take then that is what I will have to do," I responded.

"What does taking her have to do with you anyway?" the woman asked.

"Because, she's my friend. No, because I care a lot about her. Now send her out to me or I will have to kill you all even though I don't want that," I threatened.

The woman laughed, "So you think you can take us all on, you may have fought my daughter and son but don't go thinking you are any match for me," she said defiantly.

"I don't think, I am very sure of it. I didn't come looking for a fight. This can be avoided, give Lana to me and I will let you and your family be. Keep her and you leave me no choice. Either way, I will have what I came for." I said.

"Well, I've got news for you. Lana is home now. She's not yours to have. She's my daughter, she was taken away from me by her father. Who I understand is dead now? And now we have found her and she will not leave us again," the woman declared.

My eyes furrowed in confusion, I don't believe her; they probably killed her and want to be rid of me.

"I don't believe you, send her out and let her tell me that herself."

"We will do no such thing. Lana is resting. Those boys that you set free, were going to harm her, they took her to the field and were pushing her about tugging at her clothes. If we hadn't got there on time, who knows what could have happened. Where were you then, when she needed you? We protected her not you, now run along little wolf, there's nothing here for you."

"Like I said, I will leave when Lana asks me to. If I don't see her, it's trouble for all of you."

I saw the boy give his mum a quick glance and before I knew it, he leapt up into the air and changed his form. I was prepared, I changed and met him mid-air and we both tumbled to the ground. I quickly got back up on my fours and placed his neck in the grip of my mouth and yanked him towards his mother's feet. I was bigger than she had expected, I could see the fear in her eyes as I moved closer towards her with my tail high in confidence. Her daughter changed and attacked me immediately. I heard their mother shout, "No Dina! Don't fight!" but it was too late.

I yanked her out of the way like I did her brother. I heard her land with loud moan. I was waiting for the mother to change, as I wasn't going to fight her in her human form. Hearing her son and daughter whimpering on the floor, she changed her form to my surprise. I didn't want to hurt the whole family but they were giving me no choice.

Her son and daughter both flanked me on my sides. I knew this was it, no more playing, I would be going for the kill. I was going to attack the mother first to deter the other two. I didn't wait for her to attack before leaping at her. She fought me more vigorously than the other two had done. You could tell she was no novice to fighting but my size and strength outmatched hers and gave me the advantage. It was not easy, I felt the other two biting away at me, but I didn't let their attack stop me. I opened my mouth wide and was about to go for the kill when I heard Lana's voice.

"Harry don't!" I immediately turned my head in her direction and from nowhere I felt someone hit me in the head, centring my gaze on Lana's face as it blurred away. I went into oblivion.

Walking up, I had unconsciously changed back into my human form. I heard people arguing.

"Why did you hit him?" it was Lana's voice that pierced through me, and just then, I knew I had a horrible headache.

"Your boyfriend was going to kill our mother," Dina defended.

"You don't know that for sure, Harry is not like that," Lana said.

"Don't worry about it now. We are all well. The fight was pointless anyway. But he, he is a rarity. Wolves that grow as big as him are called superiors. Do you think he knows what he is? Lana's mother said.

"Superiors!?" Jonah exclaimed. "I have heard of such wolves but I thought they said they don't exist anymore. How come he is one? I could have guessed the other day, the way he took us on like we were nothing. I don't think we should be here when he wakes up. He will kill us all," Jonah protested.

"He won't harm you. The fight could have been avoided if you had let me see him," Lana argued her point.

"Well, it's all in the past now. Let's hope we don't have to fight again. Not that I would."

I pretended as though I didn't hear anything they said, as I took in what Lana's mum just referred to me as. It was weird thinking of her as Lana's mum. That meant I had been wrong to have picked fights with them. I never want any harm to come to Lana and that included her family as well. If Lana was one of us, then Mum didn't have anything to worry about. I wondered if she knew about any of this or if she just found out the truth. This meant her father lied to her about her mother walking out of her life.

I deliberately moved my body so they could see I was awake.

"Harry!" Lana came to my side, while the other three stood a distant away.

I opened my eyes, and saw her beautiful face and smiled.

"Are you alright? How's your head?" Lana asked concern etched on her face.

"I will live, but I could do with some painkillers." I said. She made to go and I held her hand close to stop her from leaving.

"What is it Harry?" she asked. "Do you need something, food, water?"

"No! I just... I'm glad you're okay." I said and released her hand.

Then she left. I tried to get up and saw that I had on someone else's clothes. I knew I must have destroyed mine while we fought.

Looking at the other three, I squinted my eyes and said, "I'm sorry if I hurt any of you." There was a short silence, then the mum spoke, "It's okay. You came because you care for my daughter, I respect that in any man or wolf."

"Still, I see she's not afraid of any of you, and looking closely now I can see the resemblance. She's lucky you were there to protect her from those goons."

"That's fine," she said and gestured for the others to leave the room.

When she was sure no one was around, she came towards me. "May I?" she asked gesturing to the seat close to me, I nodded. "So, what now?"

I looked from her to the space in front of me. I didn't know how I was going to live without Lana. I was in love with her even though I had not summoned the courage to tell her, but she was home now and there was not much I could do about it.

"I don't know, I guess it's really up to Lana now. If she likes it here with you then I shall leave, but if she chooses to come with me, then I will not leave without her." I said.

She was quiet.

"It's a long story, how I came to lose my daughter. Her father stole her away at night. But I don't intend to let go of her again but as you said, it is up to her. After all she is my daughter not my prisoner." She paused and waited for me to say something, when I didn't, she continued. "We don't have to be enemies; I like how you care for her. You know where we are now, and I'm guessing you are not far off. If she decides to stay, she knows how she can see you if she wants to and if she goes, she knows where we are," she said and patted me gently on my hand.

"I couldn't have put it better myself," I said.

She smiled.

Just then, Lana walked in with a glass of water and some pills. Her mother excused us, I waited for her to go out of hearing range.

"So, you look well," I said

"You don't look half as bad," she joked.

I swallowed the pill. Then looked at her, "Did you hear all that?" I asked.

Lana looked down, "Yes, I did."

"And?"

"I don't know, she's my mother that's for sure. I mean look at Dina, we look like we could be twins. Plus, she showed me baby pictures and pictures of all of us with my dad before he stole me away.

"Anyway, I'm glad you found your family, I know how important family is to you. I'm glad you had us, and now you have them."

"Who says I can't have the two?"

"I don't understand."

"Harry, I'm sorry I left. I didn't understand, I couldn't get my head around it. I know your mum must be really disappointed in me. And I'm really very sorry."

"Don't worry about it, I will explain everything to mum. She will understand."

I looked at her, "I'm sorry I didn't tell you about myself. I was afraid it would ruin everything but it came out anyway. Even though I promised mum that I wouldn't tell you. That kept me from telling you how I feel about you."

"Harry…"

"Wait, let me finish. I'm in love with you Lana. I think from the very first day I saw you, I knew you were the one for me. And I was a coward about it. I'm sorry. You don't have to say anything now, or tell me anything. I just wanted you to know."

"Well, nothing's changed for me really, I love you too. I think you already know that."

I smiled. "So now what?"

"Now you go back to your mum, I need to get to know mine but you are welcome to visit every day. In fact, I insist upon it."

I smiled, and grabbed her and my lips fell upon hers and before we knew it, we kissed for ages like our lives depended upon it.

"My hero," Lana whispered as we stopped for breath.

"Alright, enough you two, it's late. I think Harry needs to get back home before his mother sends out a search party." I giggled as I got to my feet. "You're right, I promised her I will be home for dinner," I said and stole another quick kiss.

"Then I guess you need to hurry home."

I smiled with content, "Yeah you're right."

"I will see you tomorrow after breakfast." I said to Lana,

"And thanks for the change of clothes," I said to Jonah, "and sorry for before."

Jonah smiled, "Don't sweat it."

Then I turned to Dina, "I'm really sorry for the other day and today. Misconception really," I said holding my hands in the air.

"Just hurry and go home," Lana said, "See you tomorrow."

"Yeah see you… Lana."

I was on cloud nine as they say, I began jogging home. I had never been this happy. Lana loves me. I always knew it but now there was no more worries. We can be together without secrets and Mum can sleep at night without worrying that Lana will tell on us.

When I got home, I found mum at the front door. I had worried her. She drew me to her and wrapped her arms around me like I was still a thirteen-year-old boy before I was turned.

Then she pulled away and looked at me.

"And? Did you find her? I sensed you were in trouble, what happened?" So many questions coming at me from her. I didn't know where to begin and I didn't have it in me to start recounting everything step by step.

"Mum, I will tell you everything in the morning. Right now, I just want to eat and sleep. I'm exhausted," I said as I stepped inside our hallway.

Mum could tell she wouldn't get anything out of me now. "Okay, I'm just glad you're home but you must tell me everything in the morning," she warned.

"Of course. By the way, I know I said I can't tell you everything now but just so you know, Lana is fine. She's with her family now and, before you say it, our secret is safe." I said over my shoulder.

"But Harry... how can you be sure?"

"Mum, I just told you that to ease your worry. You will know more tomorrow. Trust me," I said and entered into the kitchen. It didn't take me long to locate my already plated food in the oven.

I picked a fork and had a mouthful.

"Wow! Delicious," I mouthed as I ate and remembered the declaration of love between me and Lana and my heart raced inside me with happiness.

Mum entered the kitchen and saw me grinning foolishly.

"Someone's happy," she mentioned.

"Yeah!" I said, "this food is out of this world."

"Thanks, I will take the complement but I'm sure there is more to your foolish grin."

"No, I just love you, the food is great and I found Lana. I'm just happy cause everything is great in the world," I said as I continued to chow down the food.

I downed a glass of water. Kissed mum goodnight and went to my room to relive the kisses with Lana all over in my head until sleep caught up with me.

# Chapter 16

## The Return of James Stein

At breakfast, I told mum the whole story minus the declaration of love bit and the kissing bit, plus oh! I deliberately omitted the part where Evie and her gang of friends got involved.

Her mouth formed a big o, "Wow! So, she's one of us then? We really don't have anything to worry about anymore with regards to Lana now."

"Yeah! I knew we could trust her anyway. She loves us, she wouldn't have done that to us," I defended.

"Well, I had a little worry but, I'm glad she's finally back where she belongs. Just let her know, that I expect to be seeing her too. She may not be mine but I loved her like she was."

"I will definitely let her know. I will be going over to hers later today. I mean, after breakfast," I said.

Mum raised her brow, "Don't you think that is a bit too early. Lana needs time to adjust to her family. What she doesn't need is you prancing about like you own her. I don't think her family will like that either."

"They don't mind, they told me I was welcome anytime." I said.

"Did they really! Well, what did you expect them to say, after you almost killed their mother? I don't think you should go there today. Give it some time, a day or two and then go back."

"Ah, I don't know. I don't think Lana would like that, she will be expecting me and I don't want to let her down."

"Is there something you are not telling me Harry Moon?"

"What! No!" I lied.

"I told you everything already," I said looking down at my plate.

"Really?"

"Well, not really," I said because I hated lying to my mum. "I kinda told her, I love her," I muffled the words out.

"You love Lana? Is that what I heard you say. I mean, I should have known the two of you were close and then not, I knew you were fond of her but to say you love her. How would you know?"

"I do know, I have known for a long time, and she loves me too and I know we are young but we care for one another. Before I wasn't going to pursue things with her, what with our secrets and her being just a human, but now that is not in the way anymore. She is like us, at least her family is, even if she is not. We can marry, be together start a family of our own," I said proudly.

"Okay, you need to slow it down a minute Mr Love Puppy. You don't even know she wants to marry you. I mean, you are only 17. You don't have your education yet, how are you going to support her? I think you should enjoy being together now and sort your future out, and who knows maybe in five years' time we will revisit the topic of marriage."

"Well, I wasn't talking about marrying her now. But I see my future with only her, is what I was trying to explain."

"Okay Harry Moon, let's hope she feels the same way. I don't want you to get your hopes up, or get your heart broken."

"She feels the same way Mum; I mean not about marriage but the other one."

"I don't understand."

"Mum, she said she loves me too, and then we kissed," I explained.

"Oh, okay, too much information. I'm happy for you. I know what it feels like to be in love so young, remember you both have promising futures so when expressing your love for one another be sensible, and just keep me updated on a need to know basis or if you need advice on buying her gifts, you know to do that you will need to have money."

"I know mum, it's still early days though."

Mum laughed, "Forgive me, aren't you the one already talking about marriage. Anyway, just promise me you will be careful especially around her family. We don't know them at all and… Just be careful," Mum warned, then got up.

"Before you leave home, the tutor I got for you will come tomorrow. I need you to be here with him, and I'm looking into opening a book shop on the high street, since we will no longer be running away. So maybe you can come work for me after your lessons and earn a bit of cash. After all, you have a girl to spoil rotten now," Mum added and I laughed. She went upstairs.

I want to leave but mum had said to give her space, so I reluctantly stayed in my room until the evening came. I could smell mum's cooking but my heart and body were itching to see Lana.

"I will see you later mum, going to see Lana," I called out before shutting the front door close.

I half jogged into the woods, then I felt the hair on the back of my neck raise. I turned around carefully, and saw James and his dad. I couldn't believe who I was looking at, and I wondered what they were doing here in the woods so close to Lana's house.

"James Stein, is this really you?" I questioned, and then felt a punch to my face from nowhere. My eyes saw double, and the next thing I knew, my face was flat in the dirt. I woke up feeling woozy as I was being dragged away. I didn't understand why they attacked me. If anything, I thought they should have been the ones on the receiving end of my fist.

I felt drugged, so much for the excitement I had earlier to see Lana. It didn't look like anyone would find me again if these two ever got away with their intentions for me. Which now, I was wondering about seriously.

Pretending to be out of it still, I overhead them argue amongst themselves.

"You don't know that he is a superior, dad."

"Mata will never lie to me. She saw him and we cannot have a superior amongst us calling the shots and ruling the pack," James' dad argued.

"Even if he is, you don't know him like I do. He will make a good superior like you said, it is a calling. There haven't been any superiors in centuries. Why do you want to kill him? He is a rarity and he was my friend even if I had not been a good one to him."

"Listen he has to die; superiors can only come from our blood. He isn't our blood, yes you scratched him but we can't have an anomaly. He will spoil everything and every pack will think they can do as they please."

"He may be our blood; you don't know that. Why don't we investigate."

"There's nothing to investigate. My brother was meant to be the next superior but he died years ago, the next one will either come from any other child I have or you have. He must die." James' dad said, and pulled out his knife.

"No dad, I can't let you kill him. It's murder."

"I bloody don't care, now move out of the way. I am your alpha; I command you to obey."

"And if I don't?"

"Then you leave me no choice boy, I will have to kill you too if that is what it takes."

"I won't let you kill him!" James said defiantly.

"Then I'm sorry boy," his dad said, swinging his knife at James.

Then out of nowhere, he turned, there was silence at first, then the sound of a twig breaking and then a wolf appeared from nowhere and leapt at him, pulling him by his neck and then tearing out his throat. It was quick and swift; I had never seen anything like it before. James' father shook on the ground until life seeped out of him.

I opened my eyes, as strength began to return to my body. I saw the wolf run to my side in quick defence, I had heard the argument between James and his father and was glad I had him to look after me. But knowing that

I knew now that Lana's family had something to do with James's dad wanting to kill me made me worry. The talk of me being a superior had played on my mind all night. I mentioned it briefly to my mum and gauged if she knew anything about it, but she said nothing. But the wolf that came to my defence was more than familiar, she was my mother. She must have sensed that I was in trouble.

James quickly ran to his father's side. I wasn't sure if he was going to try and avenge his father even though his father had declared he would kill him to get to me. I sat up, feeling my full-strength return.

"Thanks Mum," I said.

"You're welcome," I heard her say into my mind. I walked towards James; Mum sneered.

"It's alright, Mum, he's just lost his dad," I said

I stood a distance away, and saw him looking down at his father's body.

"I'm sorry," I said,

"You have nothing to be sorry for, it's not your fault."

"Still, I owe you my life," I said.

"No, you don't. This wouldn't have happened if we didn't come here. I don't know if I can say that he deserved it but he believed in the things he stood for. And I had no say in any decisions he made. But not anymore, I couldn't just let him murder you, when you did no wrong," he said, still not looking away from his father's body.

I didn't know what to say.

"I'm sorry I left you," he turned to face me, "It was not my decision. I wanted to be there for you, to explain things to you but my father would not have any of it. He said if you couldn't survive on your own then you were not meant for this world. But look at you, you more than survived. You are a superior," he said and bowed his head.

"C'mon, what are you doing? Stop it."

"I can't, all alphas must bow to the superior. Even if they don't want to, it is inbuilt. My father dying means I am now the alpha to our pack and I can only look up if you command it so," he explained.

"Okay, I command it so. Please look up," I said casually.

"Well what now?" he asked

"What do you mean by that?" I questioned.

"I see no one has taught you about the authority a superior has, and why would you know, I abandoned you. If you want, I can stay with you and teach you until you are well versed. All alphas will hear about you and your life will be in constant danger until you know the power you have, only then will they all be pots in your hands. But to understand how you are a superior, we must first understand who your father is. We have to find him," he said.

I looked from him to mum who I knew heard everything that James just said. I wasn't sure how open mum would be to the idea of finding my father but I couldn't have the silence on the topic of my father from her any longer. This superior situation was all new to both of us but if we must survive all the other alphas that will come fighting, then it must be done.

I was in a state, only just minutes away from Lana. If mum had not come to my aid, I could have died here and she would have never known it. There was no more time to waste, Lana's family couldn't be trusted and

I had to tell her now to get away from them and come with us.

"Thanks, James," I said also noticing that he had grown much taller than when I last saw him.

"Okay, go back with mum to our house, I need to be somewhere. I will meet you at home," I said.

Walking over to Lana's mum's cabin, I was fuming inside but for Lana I knew I wouldn't hurt them. I knew Lana's mum was behind it, she didn't want me taking her daughter again so she sent James' father after me to kill me. Only she knew what I was, she didn't know I heard her but she made a very big mistake crossing me like she did.

On reaching the cabin, I saw Lana run out to meet me. I tried to smile for her sake and kept my anger hidden within me. My fight was with her mother alone. I saw how shocked her mother was to see me and I could have pretended but I had no time to beat about the bush.

"Surprised I'm alive?" I blurted out.

She laughed nervously, "Whatever do you mean Harry?"

"You know what I'm talking about," I said

"What's happening here," Lana looked from me to her mother.

"Yeah, why don't you tell your daughter what you did?"

"What is he talking about?"

Jonah and Dina appeared out of nowhere.

"Look, it's not what you think. I didn't know what he was going to do. I take it you've met him?"

"Met who? Can you stop talking in circles and explain to me what is going on?" Lana said.

"Well, your new family here, sent James' father to kill me," I declared.

"What!" Lana jumped up. "Is it true?"

"No Lana wait, I can explain. I just wanted him to know about him, there is only one family that superiors come from. So, I called around, to see if he was one of them."

"But you knew if they didn't claim him as one of theirs, they would kill him," Dina chimed in,

"I wasn't to know that, I just wanted to know what family he belonged to," Lana's mum said defensively. "I mean, he is with my daughter, and if they are to be seeing each other, I wanted to be sure that she was in safe hands," she explained.

Lana's eyes clouded with tears, "In safe hands, what if he had died, would you have ever told me you had something to do with his death? Who do you think took me in when father died? I couldn't be in more safer hands. Instead of you showing him and his mum gratitude for their help you set a big dog after him. I must be out of my mind thinking I can stay here and we can pretend like we are family. You may have given birth to me but make no mistake, you are not my family," Lana declared.

"Lana, please don't speak like that. There's still a lot I have to teach you, I need you to understand that I wasn't to know what will befall him. Look at him, he is a superior. No alpha can take on a superior. If I thought he would be in any danger, I would never have done what I did," she protested.

"I don't believe you," Lana said harshly.

"I don't either," Dina said, "But I know that you love Lana and you may have gone about things the wrong way but ultimately, you wanted to keep Lana safe."

Lana's mum's eyes clouded with tears and I felt terrible for having caused a rift between mother and daughter. I could have dealt with all better I thought.

"Lana, we love you. Mum had been depressed ever since dad took you away. Please for the sake of our family, give us all a second chance. We won't fail you, please. You are my sister, and I am only just getting to know you, don't go, stay I beg you," Dina pleaded.

"I don't know if I can," Lana said.

I took a deep breath in; I had caused this and I had to be the one to fix it.

"Lana, listen to your sister. Your mum may have been misguided in her protection of you but she is your mum and I will like to believe she loves you. My mum killed the alpha that attacked me today to keep me safe. That is what mum's do. Don't leave because of me, I beg you. Give them another chance," I pleaded with her, she smiled.

"C'mon, lil' sis, we love you," Jonah added.

"Okay then, I will stay but anymore shenanigans like this and I'm gone."

"Thank you, I promise, I won't ever do anything like that. I see now how much he means to you and as you are my daughter, he has become my son too and I shall protect him as such," Lana's mum reassured. Everyone was quiet, then she turned to me and added. "Please, Harry accept my apology."

"It's okay, I'm still breathing so no harm done really." I said casually.

Lana smiled; I could tell she wasn't as upset anymore. I extended my hand to her and she locked arms with me.

"Alright then, I have to go, I will come back tomorrow, and we can go on a hike together," I said as Lana and I began walking out of the cabin together.

"I will come with you, sleep the night. I need to see your mum anyway and apologise," Lana said loudly so her family could hear her.

"Oh! Can I come too?" Dina asked, "I don't like being cooped up here in this cabin and before you say it, I'm not coming along to spy on you. I would actually like to meet Harry's mum too; she took care of you. I would like to thank her for being a mum to you, when you needed one."

"Well then," I said shrugging, "I don't mind, Lana what do you think?"

"Yeah sure, you can come with us, if you want."

"I want to very much," Dina said happily. "Just wait a moment, let me take a change of clothes for the two of us. As I understand, Lana lost her belongings, so she will share my clothes until she gets her own." Dina explained and went to pack.

"Well maybe one day, you will take me and mum to meet your mum too Harry," Jonah mentioned.

"Yeah, one day," I said.

He smiled at Lana. "Well lil' sis, don't stay away for too long. I love having you around," he said. Lana smiled and then he exited the room.

"Lana, don't stay away too long, my darling. We still have a lot more catching up to do," Lana's mum said. Lana did not respond. It was still too soon to forgive her mum but at least she was no longer as upset as she was earlier. Then her mum turned to me. "One more time Harry, I apologise," she said and gave us privacy. I waited until her mum was no longer in the room and then I pulled her close.

I couldn't wait to get my arms around her. "I missed you," I said

"I missed you too," she responded. I wanted so badly to kiss her again, but I knew Dina would be out soon and I didn't want to be doing that in front of her family.

Just then, Dina came out as I had guessed and the three of us set out for my house.

# Chapter 17

## Lana the white wolf

We walked silently holding hands as we walked through the woods to my house. There were a lot of things I wanted to tell Lana, but they were things I didn't want to share with Dina around.

Soon we were home. I reluctantly let go of her hand and followed behind slowly as Lana and Dina made their way into the house.

"Wow! This is lovely. Your home is beautiful," Dina complimented.

"Thank you," echoed Lana and I.

It made me happy that she still considered our house as her home.

"Everywhere is so big," Dina continued.

Just then mum appeared with James in toe.

Until then I had forgotten about James. As he approached, something felt off, and I immediately saw how his eyes drooled on Lana. It made me rage inside, but I didn't want to show Lana that James staring at her the way he did bothered me, plus James saved my life earlier, beating the hell out of him was not the way to say thank you.

"Hello, Mum," I said, my eyes still not leaving James. I wondered if I should use my superior authority on him and command him to leave as the way he stared at Lana made me too uneasy. I had hoped he would notice the way I glared at him and stop his staring assault on Lana. By now everyone in the room must have noticed how stupidly and nonchalantly he stripped her down with his eyes.

My mum cleared her throat, as she could tell that James' behaviour bothered me.

"Lana, it's good to see you again. Are you staying now?" Mum asked.

"Yeah! Just for the night. I didn't… I didn't like how I left… I don't know what I was thinking when you've been nothing but caring. I'm sorry I left the way, I did. Just please forgive me."

"Don't worry about it. Just glad you are well. And who is this? Wait, don't tell me; I can see the resemblance. She's your sister, right?"

"Yeah you're right. I wonder if you won't mind her staying with me for the night?" Lana asked.

"No, not at all, your family are now my family, Lana. That's how much you mean to us." Mum said and smiled at Dina. "I'm Christina, you may call me Christy for short and your name is?"

"Dina," Dina responded.

"What a beautiful name? Well then, welcome, Dina and make yourself at home. "

"Thank you. I appreciate this," Dina said.

"Alright then, since there are more of us tonight, I better go make sure I can feed you all," Mum said.

"Do you need help?" Dina asked.

"Well if you are offering, who am I to turn it down. Come with me," she replied.

She and Dina made their way to the kitchen, leaving Harry, Lana and James alone in the hallway.

Lana could tell there was tension in the air, anyone with eyes could see how James stared at her and it felt like he wanted her to swallow her whole and it made her uncomfortable.

To let James, know that he didn't have a chance with her, Lana moved closer to Harry and placed her arms around his waist breaking James' spell. He looked away immediately as though he couldn't bear to watch her with Harry.

Without saying anything, Harry and Lana began walking up the stairs.

When they were out of hearing range, Harry opened the door to his room and Lana stepped inside. Even though they had lived together this was really the first time Lana had come into his room.

When she was in the middle of the room, she turned around to face Harry who still stood at the entrance to his door.

"Why don't you shut the door and come join me?" Lana said.

I half smiled and obliged, moving towards her, I felt my heart race inside me.

I always knew she was beautiful, but watching her now, I felt like the luckiest man in the world.

As I stood facing Lana, our heads almost touching, I delicately placed my hands on her waist and she did the same. I could feel my body shake at her touch. I wanted to kiss her, I thought about asking her but I could see in her eyes that she wanted the same.

Lana's lips parted slightly, I took it as an invitation and joined my lips with hers. Closing my eyes and letting the explosion of feelings combust inside me as our lips circled around each other.

Lana pressed her body against mine, and I raged inside with the need to touch her but I resisted the urge. Breaking away, not because I didn't want to kiss her but because of the need for more.

I held her face in my hands and planted a kiss delicately on her forehead.

"I know I told you before, but I need you to know again. I love you Lana, I'm so in love with you, you don't even know the half of it."

Lana wanted to say something, but I stopped her.

"Shush, you don't have to say anything, I just wanted you know my heart and to really apologise for those times that I couldn't tell you exactly how I felt for fear of losing you."

Lana smiled, "I'm so happy."

"I want you to be, I want to be with you always, I never want to part from you and I know you have your family now... I just..."

"It doesn't change anything, Harry... you know I feel exactly the same. You and I, we are one, I don't want to be away from you either especially now that I know you love me as much as I love you. If we weren't so young, and you asked me to marry you, I would." Lana declared.

My eyes lit up, "Really!"

"Yeah!" Lana said.

I got on his knees, "Well Lana, I don't have a ring for you now, but who needs one when we are both caught in a ring of love. I don't think how I feel about you will change; I know that in my heart but only time will prove it. No one else will ever come close to how you make me feel Lana, of that I can assure you. So, marry me, just say yes you will and it doesn't have to be now, it's just a promise that when we both are old enough and able to put a roof over our heads, we will do this with our love still burning strong. Marry me Lana." I professed.

"Harry…" Lana got on her knees and held Harry's hands

"You know I…."

Just then my door busted open, I turned my head in the direction of the noise. James walked briskly into the room and pulled Lana up to her feet.

"I'm sorry, Harry, I can't let you take her," James-said.

"What are you talking about?" I said, enraged

at James' audacity to storm into his room and handle Lana the way he just did.

"Let go of me!" Lana screamed.

"I'm sorry," he said to Lana, gripping her tightly.

"You don't belong with him. I know you think you love him but I know what I felt when I saw you. You are mine, and I need to prove that to you," he said as he gripped her arms tightly.

"Let go of her now!" I commanded; my voice became thunderous.

"Sorry, I can't do that. I have a pull to her, and your superior authority can't overrule that. When you've been at this wolf thing as long as I have, you will understand that she isn't yours to have." James declared.

"Don't I have a say in the matter?" Lana shouted. "You bull, I don't want you, I want Harry. Does that count, is that not simple enough for you to understand."

"I'm sorry but you don't have a say in this. You will come to understand this soon. You are mine and I claim you as my life partner."

Before Harry and Lana could get their heads around what James was saying, James quickly changed his form and bit Lana on her leg.

Lana screamed out in agony. Dina and my mum rushed into the room after the noise of the commotion reached them in the kitchen.

"What's happening here?" Mum demanded.

There was no time to explain things to them, I needed to deal with James quickly. I leapt up, and changed my form in a bid to fight him.

Dina rushed to her sister and placed the scarf she had wrapped on her arm on Lana's wound.

No one understood what was going on.

"Stop fighting," Mum shouted but James and I, were beyond reasoning with. I towered above James but James held his ground.

"The bleeding won't stop, if I don't take her to my mum now, she may die!" Dina shouted out.

Harry's mum didn't know what to do. Harry and James were fighting. She needed that to stop so they could get to the bottom of things and she had to also drive Lana to her mum so she doesn't bleed to death.

"Harry, hear me now, stop, she's dying. We have to go now or she will die here!" Mum shouted.

"You two can deal with each other later, but we have to get Lana help."

I stopped at once, and whined. I walking decisively towards Lana where she laid on the floor with Dina by her side, and I placed my head on her chest.

"I know you're hurting, but we need to go now," Dina said to hurry me along.

Lana placed a feeble hand on my fur as she whispered into my ears, "I will marry you Harry."

I stepped away as Dina and my mum tried to carry Lana down the stairs. James changed back to his human form and without permission he slipped into one of my shorts and shouted, "She will die before you get there, I can help."

"No!" Lana said weakly, "No, not him, he did this." Lana protested.

"She doesn't want your help," Dina said out loud.

"Nobody wants your help," I added, having changed my form too.

"Then she will die," James stated.

"If she dies, you die," I promised, walking towards Lana.

"I mean it, if you take her to wherever you are going, nothing they do will save her. Only I can, I claimed her as my own when I did that to her and only the venom from my spit can heal her," James said and enjoyed the shock on my face when what he was saying registered.

"What are you saying?" I asked again.

"You're not a fool, you understand perfectly what that means," James said.

I felt blood rush to my head and I wanted James dead but I knew if I did that, if what James was saying was true, then I had condemned Lana to death.

Tears flowed from my eyes,

"It's true." Dina said, he has to kiss her wound, that's the only way she will heal," Dina confirmed.

"And then what?" I asked.

"And then… she…. she…" Dina couldn't complete her sentence.

"Please tell me, Dina! What happens after he heals the wound…please?"

"She will belong to… to him," Dina said.

"No!" Lana said weakly.

"I would rather die… Harry no, I don't want that," she mumbled.

"I can't let you die, Lana." My tears spilled onto Lana's face as I held her to me. "I can't watch you die. Please, Lana, as much as it kills me to say this, we need him to heal you," I wept.

"But then, I won't be able to be with you…" Lana whimpered.

"We will find a way, Lana. But first, you must live for us, for me, for you, my love. You must stay alive."

My mum could see the pain James had brought me.

"If Lana didn't need you, I would have cut you down where you stand now. Now go and heal her, she must not die," Mum said. James smiled, amused with himself.

"I need room," he said as he got closer to Lana.

"No," Lana held my hand, "I don't want him near me. Harry, no!"

"We don't have a choice, my love. He has to do this," I said, reluctantly releasing Lana's hands.

I stepped away and turned my back not wanting to see what James was doing.

As James bent over the wound, he looked at Lana and said, "Forgive me, this was a necessary evil. I had to do this to seal our future."

"I don't want you; I don't love you and I never will." Lana said.

"Yes, yes, for now. But soon after you are healed, you won't have a choice and together we will raise our family. You will love me. I can promise you that," James told her, then he ripped the clothing from around the wound, giving him room to work before drooling his spit all over the open flesh.

Lana screamed in pain. I held my head as the agony she was going through and the realization that I had lost her to James cut through me.

It felt like ages, but it only took a few minutes for James to complete his ritual.

Mum held on to me, my body shook in rage and she needed to calm me down. Dina held Lana's hands as her eyes rolled in their sockets with each kiss James planted on her body as he claimed her as his own.

When it was all done, James said, "She will live, but she now belongs to me. I will go now but I will be back for her." And then taking one last look at Lana, he walked down the stairs and out of the house.

No one knew what to say. I wanted to go to Lana, but I didn't know if I had a right to still feel as strongly as I did for her now that James had claimed her as his.

The silence was deafening.

"I will take Lana home now, it's only right. I don't think we can stay here anymore," Dina said.

No one responded. I didn't want her gone; but I knew I couldn't bare it if suddenly Lana started to yearn for James.

"My body is burning up," Lana said.

I ran to her side at once, "Lana, are you okay?"

"No, Harry, I'm not. I'm burning inside." Lana had turned red.

"What did he do her?" I looked at Dina for answers.

"Claiming her as his own triggered her wolf genes. She is changing."

I remembered how badly it hurt the first time I turned and it was because of James Stein and now he had done the same to Lana, leaving her alone to carry the pain.

"Breathe, my love," I comforted her.

"I can't, I'm dying; I feel like I'm dying," Lana groaned as the agony took hold of her whole body.

Just then, I noticed that where James had bitten Lana before was all healed.

"Help me, Harry, take it all out. I don't want James, please help me. Take out his poison from inside me."

"I don't know how to, Lana."

"Please, Harry, don't condemn me to this fate," Lana yelled in pain.

"Harry, you are a superior, whatever you do, you can overrule James. Just think, it will come to you naturally. Help her!" Dina uttered holding Lana's hands.

"Just think, Harry, help her," Mum added.

I closed my eyes, and held Lana.

"I will take the pain away, my love."

I placed my mouth over Lana's, as though commanding all that James introduced into her out of her. Lana began to sweat all over her body as James' fluid in her began to answer to my will. I closed my eyes as James' venom burned in my mouth. Overriding James' power over her, I spat out the venom and sat down in exhaustion next to Lana.

Lana seemed more calmer now but she was clearly still in some pain.

"I don't understand," I turned to Dina. "I took it all out."

"Yes, you took out James' claim on her but she is still turning and that no one can stop," Dina explained.

"Oh! So, what can I do to help?"

"I'm afraid there's nothing any of us can do. She has to do this on her own. If she survives it, then she will be a wolf like all of us," Dina explained.

"Okay, let's take her to her room," Mum said.

I lifted her off the floor and took her to her room.

They took shifts cooling her body down as Lana went through different phases of pain all night until the following day and then the next night came until the third morning greeted them. Lana was no better. Her pain got worse. I was afraid she was going to die, that she wouldn't make. My eyes were tired from lack of sleep, but I refused to eat anything or sleep until Lana was okay.

"Lana's mum is here, Harry," My mum announced.

"Okay. Does she want to come inside," I asked faintly not wanting to disturb Lana.

Mum nodded. I reluctantly left her side.

"Don't worry, Harry, I have prepared something that will help her. Her humanity is fighting the change, plus what she went through before that is stopping her brain. I will give her something and she will sleep. When she wakes, she will either be a wolf or not," Lana's mum explained outside the entrance to Lana's room.

"What do you mean by not?"

"I don't know, Harry, but trust that she is strong enough to overcome this."

"Let her go do this now, Lana needs this," My mum pulled me to her, but I held Lana's mum's hand and she turned to face me.

"Please help her. I need her to be okay," I pleaded.

"We all do." She said and stepped inside the room.

"Come now, Harry, you must eat or I will lose you and I can't do that, please my boy," Mum begged.

I could tell he had inflicted his own pain on his mum.

"I'm sorry you had to go through this, I will eat," I said. Mum smiled and led me downstairs to the kitchen.

After I had eaten, Dina, Jonah and their mum joined us downstairs.

"She is sleeping now," Lana's mum announced.

As much as I was relieved to hear that, I wondered what happens if she doesn't turn, I couldn't dare ask for fear of the unknown.

Everyone sat down quietly as time crawled along.

Then suddenly, they heard a loud howl.

I jumped out of my seat and ran up the stairs, as I reached the hallway to the rooms, I saw a white wolf coming out of Lana's room. I stopped in my stride to admire her; I had never seen anything so beautiful.

"Lana! You made it." I was elated. "You made it, my love." I moved closer to her, she leapt up and pounced on me and I roared out in laughter. I could hear her thoughts as well. "I made it, Harry, now nothing can separate us."

The others all stood back and watched as Harry and Lana played with each other, Lana was in her wolf form and Harry in his human form and even the blind could see that they were mad for each other.

"I have a lot to teach you, my love," I announced.

"Yeah! I can't wait. But first, I feel like running. Want to come run with me?" Lana asked.

"Sure! I hope you can catch up." I said and changed my form. We breezed past everyone, running wild into the fields.

"Take it easy Lana. I don't want you to hurt yourself."

"No, slow coach. Why would I when I can run free. Catch me if you can."

"Just wait a minute, please, Lana," I called but Lana ran faster.

She was very fast, faster than any wolf I thought. I knew she wasn't going to stop unless I made her.

"Ouch!" I yelped.

Lana ran back, "What happened, Harry? Are you okay?" I waited until she was near me.

"Okay I faked that. I'm okay really. But I needed to speak to you."

"So, you faked an injury?"

"Yeah! I'm sorry I did that."

Lana laughed. "It's okay. So what now, you want to go back home?"

"Yes, I want you to take it easy, I only just got you back." Harry said.

"Okay 'kill joy', let's go back home."

Once home, we both changed. While Lana sat in the kitchen with my mum and her family, I got inside the shower. I wanted to be with Lana alone but not in the wolf form and I was willing for her to spend time with everyone else that had also feared for her life in the last 72 hours.

"We are all just happy we have you here with us, and as you all know Lana is like my daughter so you have all become my family and my home has become your home as well. So, I guess we are all family here now." My mum said to Lana's family.

Lana turned her head as she could sense my eyes watching her, he gestured to her to come, and she got up not wanting to alert the other and followed Harry out of the house. They held hands in silence until they were far from the house.

"You gave me a scare," I confessed. "I thought... for a moment, I thought I had lost you."

"I know, I wasn't sure I was going to come out the other end too, but here we are."

"Here we are indeed," I said, as we walked. Then I moved to face her.

"I love you so much, my love."

"I love you too, my superior."

I laughed. "I don't claim you as mine, not as the wolves do, but as I was saying before, we were rudely interrupted. I wanted to wait until we were older to marry you but I think now that I can't bear to lose you and I want to start living my life with you, if you want me as I want you."

"Actually, I was the one that was rudely interrupted. Harry, I will marry you tomorrow, tonight if we could." I smiled

"If anything, people like James showed me that we don't need plans, tomorrow is not guaranteed. Let's just live life moment to moment and in this moment and I hope to do so forever, I choose you to be my husband Harry Moon." Lana declared as she moved closer to me, her heart pounding in her. I swallowed hard, admiring her beauty underneath the moon I couldn't believe how lucky he was.

"And I choose you to be my wife forever Lana." I wrapped my arms around her waist and in that moment, our lips met and our bodies melted into each other as the wind and the surrounding trees carried the tales of our magical love.

The End.

Want more books from this superbly talented author?

Then read Sebastian Vampire romance saga:

Sebastian: A Vampire's Torment,

Sebastian 2: Dark Times Arising,

Sebastian 3: Conquest of Power, and Sebastian 4: The Call of Hearts.

Other brilliant books by the author include: Hasina: My Great Escape

Jana: That Plague called Love.

Jaekeal: The Hunter Boy

And watch out for Harry Moon 2: Coming soon!

Read more about the author on her website, or visit her on Facebook, Twitter, Goodreads

www.ingramcontent.com/pod-product-compliance
Lightning Source LLC
Chambersburg PA
CBHW022114170626
46808CB00002B/721